HELL BOUND

THE GUILD OF SHADOWS 3

MARIE BILODEAU

This book is a work of fiction. Any resemblance to persons, living or dead, or places, events or locations is purely coincidental.

Cover art by Éric Belisle.

Cover design by Ânia Loureiro.

Editing by Jessica Torrance.

To Jay Odjick,
Friend and Inspiration, Storyweaver and Teller,
unapologetically One of a kind

1

CONSIDERING the glittering dresses and shiny decorations, both distracting my senses and challenging my ability to keep my shadows wrapped around me, it was a miracle I even spotted the dart before it struck the ambassador.

The real sucky part? The only way to stop the ambassador from being struck was to throw myself in front of it. Not like I had a whole lot of time to plan against a projectile. I just hoped my armor would be enough to stop it.

A sharp pain webbed out from my shoulder and heat shot down my arm and wrapped around my chest.

Well, that didn't work.

I stumbled forward, unable to stop my momentum, or that of the quickly creeping poison, and crashed into the ambassador, my shadows wrapping around him. Which meant he could see me.

Definitely not great.

His eyes grew wide at the sight of the purple demon

girl who'd just appeared beside him. Usually, I'd be mortified. But right now? I was getting so damned loopy from the poison surging through my system that I actually considered hugging him. I managed to retain some dignity.

"Hi!" I said, grinning and slipping past him. I barely even cared about how mystified he looked.

Did I just do that?

Being seen by humans was a big no-no. I was on a mission to protect the ambassador and his daughter. Other Guild of Shadows operatives weren't far, but I was the only one with the powers to hide in plain sight. Unless I got too close to humans, of course.

I stumbled past another human as the ambassador shouted in alarm.

Smooth, Tira. A dark tunnel collapsed around my vision. My shadows pulsated, trying to dissipate as my concentration slipped. Sweat trickled down my neck as I forced them to stay and protect me.

Dame Zallir would have my ass if I didn't move out of the humans' way before I reappeared completely. My heartbeat drummed in my ears, my shadows pulsing with every step as humans scrambled around me.

"Tira, what the hell is going on?" Gorsel's rough voice boomed in my earpiece, threatening to split my skull in two. I leaned against a cool, smooth wall. Nice. Except for the wallpaper, all peach and gold in a busy pattern that made my eyes cross. I poked it, my shadows dancing frantically as the (very) small part of me that was still (mostly) undrugged struggled to keep them up. Humans screamed and generally panicked, but thankfully they all managed to avoid me.

For now, anyway.

"Tira!" He screamed. I didn't like Gorsel. He was my new main partner, a large, gruff man who just happened to be made of rocks, and who could turn into a boulder (often a hairy one). As far as I knew, that was his only power.

Why the hell would they have selected someone who could turn into rocks for the Guild of Shadows? That wasn't a stealthy power.

"Not like my shadows," I'd mumbled out loud without realizing, until he replied.

"What the hell is going on?"

Oh, right. We were supposed to protect the ambassador. Well, I'd done my part. Gorsel could take it from here.

"Attack on ambassador," I said around my thick tongue. "Dart," I managed to spit out, though my mouth didn't move quite right. Why couldn't I feel my lips?

Was this thing going to kill me? I hadn't considered that. But, I supposed that since we were protecting the ambassador from assassins, that made all sorts of sense.

The light in the room grew as the din increased, and I navigated the wall, carefully following the psychedelic peach and gold pattern. Walls usually led to doors, right?

"Take an Tradenaline shot and get back in the game, Tira!"

I tried to say "screw you" but I only managed to

gurgle. Stupid Tradenaline. Basically hopped-up adrenaline shots for Traded like me, so we could keep fighting when all we really wanted to do was nap. Ian would have come up with a solid plan, not just screamed at me to pump myself full of shit.

Ian.

My shadows dropped around me for a micro-second before I managed to refocus. I didn't care about the ambassador. I wasn't even sure that I cared about the Guild of Shadows. But I cared about Ian, and I couldn't save him unless I "stayed in the game," as Gorsel so annoyingly put it.

"Fine," I mumbled, focusing on that damned wall, where the colors now danced, imagining golden ducks carrying peaches in their mouths.

That's kinda cute. And suddenly, an opening.

Finally! I almost cried with relief that the door stood ajar, not certain I could navigate a doorknob right now. I tried to maintain momentum around the corner, but the door kept moving back as I leaned against it, and I stumbled down, rolling until I landed on soft, plush carpeting.

This is nice. I stared up at the ceiling, the sparkling chandelier blinding me. My shadows trembled, afraid of the light. I'd lose them any second. I was barely able to keep my eyes open.

Not that it mattered, since I was pretty sure from my ragged breathing that I'd be dead, too.

I hate this shit, I thought as I reached with a numb finger for the infinity symbol on my left shoulder. I could barely feel the slight indentations etched in my armor. Apparently, the designers had foreseen this particular issue, and my fumbling triggered a bio scan.

A single chirp through my earpiece indicated the incoming needle.

I really hate this, I had just enough time to think before it plunged into my heart, making me scream and sit up. The dark tunnel collapsed and my vision exploded outward into light. My limbs electrified and not at all in a pleasant way as every sense went into overdrive.

The air tasted of ash, my breathing hurt, and everything was entirely too shiny.

Especially the face of the woman staring at me, wide-eyed.

Oops. I'd dropped my shadows. Despite repeated practice with this stuff (which sucked just as badly as it sounds), I still couldn't keep my shadows wrapped around me.

"Are you…" the woman started to say. I cut her off, my hyper-driven senses spotting the centipede-like intruder crawling on the ceiling.

"Down!" I leapt over her as she dropped (either because of my order or because of the purple demon now leaping toward her), pulled out my thin blade, and plunged it into the creature on the ceiling. A jet of green goo exploded from it (gross), some of the spatter landing on my arm and sizzling through the fabric.

Shit shit shit.

I grabbed the sleeve and pulled it off, just as the acid disintegrated the rest of it. Damn it. I liked that shirt.

My feet connected with the ground and I pushed

myself back up as I turned, but the creature had already fallen. It twitched as it bore a hole in the floor.

"Gross," I chucked a cryo pellet at it, ice forming around its (many, many) twitching legs, containing the acid damage.

A quick scan revealed no other enemies. At least not in the immediate vicinity.

"Stay here," I turned to the woman. She had the decency to just nod and not scream at me, wide eyes betraying her deep shock. Yeah, I guess she was having a bad day. Well, she wasn't the only one. I pulled my shadows back around me. They protested, throbbing and twitching as the adrenaline made it hard to do anything but run. So I ran as I held them close.

The next room had been emptied out. The other Guild operatives would be keeping the ambassador safe. My job had been to stop an attack in the ballroom (yay for shadow powers). Their job was to make sure he survived any subsequent attack.

Technically I was done. But I was so full of Tradenaline and Gorsel's annoying scream to "get back in the game" that I just kept running.

Right to the back of the cavernous ballroom, where I thought the dart had originated from.

No sign of anyone, so I kept running, struggling to keep my shadows around me. I burst into the back room, where staff scurried about to get the meal prepared.

I jumped up and grabbed the ceiling to avoid several servers before dropping back down, barely missing a beat.

And still I kept running.

Shit. I hated this stuff and wanted it out of my system. If I couldn't find someone else to fight, I'd damn well run it off.

I headed for the main doors, not too worried about attacks. An invisible running demon would be hard to dart. Again.

"Tira, report," Gorsel said, and I ignored him, running around another corner. Maybe I could go outside and do loops around the place. But it wasn't sunset yet, and drawing shadows from every blade of grass and stone would require so much attention…

I didn't care enough to follow through my logic and headed for the staff doors.

I would have reached them, too, had a giant fuzzy boulder not rolled into my path at the last second. Before I could swerve, I slammed right into it and flew against the wall, crumpling to the ground.

"Man, you suck at Tradenaline," Gorsel said as he shaped back into his man form.

You just suck, I wanted to say, but the impact had shocked me out of my Tradenaline rush and, between being poisoned and shot up, I was getting pretty sleepy.

"Come on," he sighed and threw me over his shoulder. I'd have complained, if I hadn't been so busy taking a nap.

2

By the time I reached my room, I was pretty sure my head had turned into a helium balloon. I hated the Tradenaline and wished it wasn't so damn useful. Or that we avoided ridiculous battles that called for its use.

Of course, since my last Guild of Shadows building had been infiltrated, destroyed, and its second-in-command captured, the stakes had skyrocketed. Our leader, Sonsil, seemed obsessed with leaving no one else behind, so equipped us with the stuff to keep us going.

That would have been a more comforting thought if the helium balloon in my head hadn't suddenly popped. Lights exploded behind my eyes and my stomach leapt into my throat. I shifted sideways, my head dangling off my bed. A bucket appeared and hands gently pulled my hair back as I puked my guts out.

"Thanks," I managed to mumble when I was done. Rachel helped me lean back onto my pillows. She sat near me, her profile outlined by the dim light of a single LED candle. Not enough light to bug me, but enough to help Rachel see.

"This sucks," I mumbled. I squinted, trying to focus on Rachel, with her blue skin and bright pink hair. Soothing pink. "How come you don't throw up when you take this stuff?"

"Everyone's different, Tira."

"Gorsel's right. I suck at Tradenaline."

"You're good at other things."

I gave a short laugh and instantly regretted it as it chiseled my skull. Every time I took the stuff, it felt like I lost time. And, over the past three weeks, I'd had many run-ins with it.

It was indispensable to help Traded keep going in the field. Like some machinery that just needed extra fuel.

Every time, I lost just a few hours, but that added up to an eternity for Ian, trapped wherever he was. *If he's still alive.* I crushed that thought with curled fists. *No.* Ian would find a way to survive. It didn't matter that it had already been weeks.

Twenty-four days.

I hated this so much. I hated that I had to keep going on missions instead of looking for Ian. He mattered more than any of this. And he'd been taken because I'd trusted the wrong Traded. *Glitter.* I'd brought him into our Guild.

I guess Ian trusted the wrong Traded, too, when he trusted me.

Fists wound tightly, I didn't even notice that I'd started to cry.

Great. Absolutely amazing.

"You'll be okay, Tira," Rachel whispered. I was about to say something pithy (I'm sure), but she kept going. "Ian will be, too. We'll find him."

I opened my eyes and focused on her, the shadows dancing on her shimmering blue skin.

"I didn't mention Ian," I mumbled.

"You're not that hard to read."

Sonsil's earlier warning danced in my drug-addled mind. *If anyone is found to be looking for him, they'll be declared rogue.*

And rogue operatives were killed. By the Watch, whatever they were.

Rachel and I hadn't hung out much since Ian had vanished and we'd both made it as operatives. I'd been out in the field so much, on what felt like an endless string of assignments. But I still considered her a solid maybe-friend, and you shouldn't get your maybe-friends killed.

"I've been looking for any sign of Ian. You're not alone in this," she said, not waiting for me to speak. Which was good, because I thought I might puke again if I tried. Listening proved challenging enough, especially since the world wouldn't stop spinning and my growing anxiety wasn't helping.

Rachel seemed to sense it and stood up from my bed. I instantly missed the comforting weight of a maybe-friend.

"I'll come by in a bit," she said softly. "You get some rest."

I wanted to stop her, but I also wanted her to go. Finding Ian would be easier with help, but Sonsil had made it amply clear that I wasn't to be found out. The more we were, the greater the chances that our attempts to find Ian would be detected.

Then again, if Rachel had already been looking, it's not like I was dragging her into anything. Not like I'd be doing with Clay.

More than three weeks had gone by since Ian had been taken, and I'd barely spoken to Clay. He'd been so busy with fights in his league, and I'd been so focused on Ian. I wanted to tell him so badly about Ian. Except he'd hated Ian, and I couldn't stand the thought of being mad at Clay for being mean about my other friend.

Before I could make up my still-foggy mind and stop her, Rachel had slipped out.

So much for stopping her.

I must have fallen asleep, because I woke up hours later as a light came on beside me. My gauntlet's display flashed, warning me of a mission brief in one hour. I sighed and pushed myself up, wishing I had more time to just wallow in bed, while simultaneously wishing I hadn't lost almost half a day already.

At least I finally felt better. I'd have to thank Rachel for taking care of me. Maybe I should re-evaluate her place on my short list of friends. People who took care of you while you were far from your best had to be friends, right?

A quick shower and a fresh set of clothes did wonders for my head, and I ducked out of my room with a few minutes to spare. I glanced to the right, wanting to go to Ian's room. It was still there, exactly as it had been since we'd moved his things from the old Guild. Because he'd come back, obviously. Neither Sonsil nor I were willing to let that particular hope go.

I'd been going there every few days to take care of his plants. I didn't know a thing about plants, but I knew they needed water. And I'd looked up a few guides on how to trim them and stuff. I sucked at it, and a bunch of them were wilting, but the vines climbing up to the cave where he slept in his various and sundry animal forms were doing well.

He'd like that.

They hadn't been tended for a few days. I was pretty sure they'd be fine, but it annoyed me. Neglecting the plants meant I neglected Ian.

But there was no time to go in there, now, with the mission briefing about to start. Just like there was no time to go over the meager evidence I'd managed to collect in the weeks since Ian vanished. And it wasn't much, no matter how big the events felt. Missing Traded. Attacks on guilds across the world. And Glitter, a trail barely leading to his past, but none to his future.

I wanted to turn in there so bad. Tending to the plants made me feel connected to Ian. Trying to find him made me feel connected to myself.

But that would have to wait for another day.

3

THE FACT that only Sonsil and Dame Zallir stood in the mission room when I entered felt like a giant spotlight straight on me. They were both rather impressive in their own ways. Sonsil's skin was dark, but lighter than Dame Zallir's. They were both about the same intimidating height. And I think they were both human, which left me in awe. Humans might say that the Traded were dangerous, but to the rest of us, it was clear that the humans were the scary ones. Because they had all the power.

Dame Zallir won out in coolness over Sonsil because 1 – she used "Dame" as a title, and 2 – she had hair while he was bald. Plus, she had recently added green streaks as a coolness bonus.

Hands down, she was the winner.

I looked back toward the door, but no one else came in. They both focused unnervingly on me.

"Glad to see you're feeling better, Ms. Misu," Dame Zallir said, and I nodded. I wanted to go on about

Tradenaline, but the way they held themselves made me think that staying quiet was my best bet.

One thing about being a Traded—you learned pretty fast when it was best to stay quiet. The tattoo on my neck, a biochemical control mechanism stamped on when I first arrived at the Margrave Academy—a "school" for Traded—suddenly itched, but I knew that was just psychosomatic.

Because it didn't itch when activated. It hurt. And it had also been dormant since I'd joined the Guild of Shadows. I guess I hadn't stepped too far out of line, yet.

"You were spotted at the ambassador's home," Sonsil said, voice low, "by a human."

I blinked, focusing on him. My tail twitched, and I forced myself to keep it under control. I hated to remind others (or myself) that I really was just a purple-skinned demon.

Neither human added anything. I took that as my cue to talk.

"I, um, to be honest, I don't really remember much of what happened."

I doubted honesty was the best policy, but it was the only policy I could apparently conjure up under pressure.

I missed Ian so bad. When he'd been second-in-command, there had been a softer place to fall.

"Let me refresh your memory," Dame Zallir said, her voice like a crisp fall day that threatened to turn to winter. "From witnesses and recorded equipment," I winced. One of those would have been bad enough, but both was super ouch, "we can tell that you took a poison dart meant for the ambassador, because you couldn't stop it any other way."

I kinda remembered that part.

"And you lost control of your shadows in front of his daughter."

Oh yes, the large eyes. Definitely remembered that.

"Then you managed to kill an acid bot targeting her, while fighting the poison."

I remembered that had been gross. And it had ruined my shirt.

"You can try to set her up as a hero all you want," a chill erupted in my spine at the familiar voice, "but she still crossed the line."

Blake walked out from behind a cabinet in the back of the room. He was good at weaseling about and impossible to ignore. His blond hair practically shone even in the dim light, his blue eyes sharp and piercing.

And cruel.

He'd made life unbearable for Clay and me when we'd been classmates at our "school." With his good human looks (so I was told), he used his popularity to bully less popular kids. And looking like a demon did *not* make me popular. Nor did Clay's refusal to give in to bullies.

"Tira," Sonsil said, either unaware of or choosing to ignore the increased tension in the room, "this is Blake Connelly, representative of the Watch."

That idiot Blake looked so proud at that statement that I plastered disinterest on my features. I hoped to hell I hid my worry and curiosity. Hell, my fear.

The Watch. The one thing that existed over all guilds, to keep them in check. Even the Guild of Shadows seemed to work for them, though I wasn't positive of that. Not yet, anyway.

"I'm just here to observe," Blake said, with none of my disinterest. Instead, he put on a show of how disappointed he was in me. "The peace between humans and Traded was hard won, after all. We'd hate to lose it because one guild's operative goes rogue."

Rogue. There was that word, again. I liked it, in theory. Sounded kinda cool and badass. In practice, though, it seemed pretty bad.

Blake took another step to stand completely in front of me. I refused to be intimated or shy away. I knew Blake wielded some form of telekinesis to freeze people in place. His more predominant power, however, the one he tended to deploy more easily and often, was his douchebaggery.

100% douchebag.

His eyes narrowed slightly. He was clearly annoyed that I didn't show him the respect, aka fear, he thought he deserved. He curled his lips, and suddenly the tattoo at the side of my neck prickled, surprising me. And, apparently, I wasn't great at hiding my surprise, a slight noise escaping my lips.

Sonsil stepped closer, getting in our space, hovering uncomfortably over both of us with his height. "We'll double how careful we are," Sonsil said, "and pull Operative Misu from the field."

Sweat curled down the side of my face as I fought against the growing pain, my lungs not quite working the way they should. I barely registered that Sonsil had called me "Operative Misu," all professional like. I guess he was trying to remind Blake we weren't unsupervised in the school yard anymore.

Only problem with Sonsil's theory was that we were still supervised, and Blake was the one doing the supervision.

"Don't pull her from the field," Blake said, though he didn't turn to Sonsil, focusing entirely on me. "Make sure you finish your mission, and no more screw ups. Or," he got closer to me, the tattoo burning so bad it took all my strength to remain standing. I refused to let my knees give way, or to reach out to Sonsil.

Like I'd let the bastard win.

"We'll make sure," Sonsil said, his voice low. "We have planning to do, if that's all." Blake waited a moment longer, holding the tattoo active, apparently too stupid to hear the threat in Sonsil's voice.

Or, a shiver ran down my spine at the realization, he knew just how powerless Sonsil was against him. And, for all my problems with the guild systems, aka fancy-sounding slavery, Sonsil tended to stand up for his people. The thought that he couldn't keep us safe from everyone freaked me out.

"Very well," Blake said, releasing the tattoo. The move was so sudden that I gasped and almost collapsed, but I managed to keep myself upright. Sonsil shifted slightly toward me, as though intending to catch me if I fell.

Without another word, golden douchebag stepped

out of the room. It was then that I realized Dame Zallir had already slipped away.

"Get some rest," Sonsil said, his attention still on the door where Blake had vanished. "You redeploy tonight. Briefing in two hours."

With that, he slipped away, too, before I'd caught my breath enough to ask him any of the dozens of questions swirling around my mind. Not even the most pressing of them all: why the hell did the Watch have the controls to my tattoo?

4

I NEEDED REST, but meeting Blake had left me twitchy, and a familiar voice would help ground me. Back when I was new to the Guild, I'd sincerely believed that getting a smart phone would help me stay connected to my oldest friend, Clay. Until I learned that our devices had so many blockers that they could only really work in the way the Guild intended for us to use them.

No connectivity in the Guild was part of it. If Guild members couldn't contact people from here, then we couldn't be tracked. And no phones in our rooms, either. Rooms were for sleeping and changing, but that was it.

As an operative, at least I had access to private booths. Private being a relative term, of course. In the Guild of Shadows, someone was *always* listening.

"Hey Tira," Jolene's sing-song voice exploded into the receiver. "Clay's just finishing up training. Want me to tell him to call you back?"

"It'll just be quick," I told Jolene. "Tell him I'm off soon, so now would be great."

If he can. I didn't add the words, their bitterness burning my throat.

"Of course, sugar," Jolene said softly. "I'll tell him." Clay was so focused on his fighting goals that he tended to forget about everything else. Including our friendship.

But he always comes through in the end.

I repeated the words like a mantra to protect our friendship.

"Hey, Tira," Clay sounded tired. He must have been training hard. Still, hearing his voice managed to make my heart skip a beat. I felt better instantly. Less alone.

"Hey, Clay," I grinned, unable to stop myself. "How'd the battle go?"

"Great!" He launched into a play-by-play, the enthusiasm managing to hold my drifting attention. He finished, breathless. "How 'bout you? How're things going?"

He wanted to ask about my mission, but he knew I couldn't talk about it. Which seriously cramped conversations and injected frustration into our friendship.

"Good!" I said, trying to sound cheerful, but knowing I was failing. "I'm good," I repeated more softly.

"Yeah?" He said, the intonation making it clear he didn't buy it. He waited, though I could hear a thousand questions begging to burst out of him. And I wanted to tell him so much.

But even what little I could tell him, I'd chosen not to. In the few moments waiting for him to come to the phone, I'd resolved not to tell him about Blake. He didn't need that distraction. It wasn't like he could help me, anyway.

"I'm going on a mission," I said. "Might be gone for a few days, so I didn't want you to worry."

A pause. An eternity.

"I always worry, Tira. You know that."

"I know. I'm sorry."

I wasn't sorry for being in the Guild of Shadows. That hadn't really been my choice. But I'd made other choices along the way, just like he had, and the secrets and tiny betrayals still echoed under every conversation.

"It's okay," he said, though I felt like I'd deflated him. "You gotta do what you gotta do."

"I worry about you, too."

"I know. And I'm sorry about that, too." Since joining his Wolf Pack League months ago, he'd climbed the ranks so fast. He had nowhere left to go in the safer categories—the ones where fighting to the death was off the table.

"That mutt better keep you safe," he said jokingly, a half-hearted attempt to lift the mood. Tears burned my eyes, sudden and unexpected. I hadn't told Clay about Ian. More than three weeks, and I hadn't told my childhood best friend that my Guild best friend was missing.

That he'd been taken, right in front of me.

Not because I couldn't tell Clay. But because I *chose*

not to. Like I wanted to keep those two pieces of my life separate. Knowing Ian and Clay disliked each other, I knew it was more than that. I couldn't risk hearing relief in Clay's voice that Ian was gone. Because I couldn't risk hating my only remaining friend.

"Don't worry about me," I rallied what perkiness I had left in me, "I'll be careful, I promise."

"Okay," another pause. "Call me when you get back? Maybe we'll even visit?"

"That would be nice." I breathed out. "Take care, Clay."

"You, too, Tira."

I hung up the phone and sighed. Sometimes, I feared my worry would bubble out of me and I'd withdraw into my shadows and never come back out.

It was the price of being Traded in this world, I guess.

Didn't matter. For now, all that mattered was the mission.

That mission, of course, was to find a way to save Ian.

5

FOLLOWING the attack on our satellite base, we'd evacuated to the main headquarters. I couldn't tell what exactly was different about it, to be honest, aside from how much *bigger* it was. Steel still lined the walls, mostly to block out attempts at electronic spying. Giant corridors spread deep underground, the entire complex like a flattened spider nested in the footprint of the city.

We could emerge easily under many important neighborhoods. Well, important to the Guild. Those areas brimming with guilds and leagues, or heavily populated by Traded. But not all corridors spread out toward them. Others were under populous city hubs, and places where humans worked and played.

Those worried me the most. Our few moments not spent training or on missions were usually fairly quiet. Most operatives had broken into groups and cliques. I didn't belong to any of them, though a few were nice enough. I just preferred not having to interact too much with them.

Not because I didn't like them. It was just that everyone seemed just as content not approaching me, either. That was fine, though, I kept trying to convince myself. If it were up to me, I'd be wrapped in shadows all the time anyway.

"Tira!" The booming voice called when I entered the mission room. My tail swished as I glared at the large lizard man who'd called after me. Rachel's new partner, Jombo, had decided we were friends since we'd arrived here. He didn't decide that about most of the other operatives, apparently, so part of me was flattered. A bigger part of me was annoyed.

"Hey," Rachel's feet were propped up on the chair in front of her as she looked over some documents on her tablet. She shot a grin my way.

"I kept you a seat!" Jombo said, and I sighed, but headed toward it. To say no to his proudly selected seat would feel like kicking a puppy. At least it was to the side and back, where I could stay out of the way. Jombo had homed in on my preferences pretty quickly after I'd almost melted at the front of the mission room. Felt like all damn eyes were on me.

Maybe Rachel had slipped him a word out of kindness to me. I liked Rachel, and really didn't want to get her into trouble. But if we teamed up to help Ian, with her smarts…

"There's Sonsil," Jombo said, leaning forward in his seat, which was just wide enough for him. Unlike our first mission room, this one was much better, with seats actually built to accommodate the many shapes and sizes of the Traded. It even had room in the back for my tail to slip out. I hated having to wrap it around me. Made it even more obvious that I was different.

In this room, I kinda fit in. Gorsel sat up front, and he turned to nod at me but didn't invite me to join him. Either he knew I would hate it up front, or he was glad I was staying away from him. There were six more operatives in the room, all of whom looked (more) human compared to us. They were the ones who could mingle with humans on missions, while I had to stay in the shadows to keep the humans—and the rest of us— safe. I remembered Blake's warning.

Glancing around at the thought of him, fear clenched at my stomach, not quite releasing when I realized he wasn't here.

Sonsil stepped to the front, an image suddenly projecting in the middle of the room. Dame Zallir was still nowhere to be seen. That was a bit weird. She'd been around quite a bit to help the new operatives settle into guild life. But who knew what she was about. I didn't think she was actually part of the Guild of Shadows. Maybe another member of the Watch? She hadn't exactly helped when Blake was here.

"Today's mission is a simple extraction," Sonsil started without flourishes or preliminaries. All heads turned to him, focusing on the images now appearing. A Traded, slightly jaundiced skin, toothy grin, mop of green hair.

"This is Jorg Loops, from the Life Trade Faction," Sonsil's face betrayed his disgust for half a second. I suspected he made sure we saw it. The Life Trade Faction wasn't a guild like us. It was little more than a circus, putting Traded on display to perform "daring feats" (aka stuff humans couldn't do). The very name sent a thousand creepy crawlies down my spine. I'd been so terrified of being sent to a circus. Me, who felt exposed just standing with other people in a room with all the lights on. That fear still clung to me.

With Ian gone, especially. He had practically handpicked me and without him, the Guild of Shadows could very well decide I was better suited to circus life.

I should probably be damned careful not to screw up again.

"Jorg went missing twenty-seven days ago," Sonsil's voice grew softer, but his words hit home. Everyone knew we'd lost one of our own twenty-four days ago. Too close to be coincidence. Rachel squeezed my hand and I realized I'd been holding my breath.

"We have a lead that he's being held here," the image changed to a city district, an old convenience store in the suburbs. *Your Luck Convenience* shone on the sign in gawdy red letters on a mustard yellow background. If I were human, I'd think this place looked pretty sketchy.

Of course, if I were as squishy as a human, I'd be cautious of most places.

"There's a basement beneath the store," Sonsil said, bringing up a building schematic. "We suspect a small but well-armed crew handles security. Our goal is to extract Jorg alive." *To find out what he knows about the missing Traded.* Sonsil didn't say it, but I was pretty sure we all understood what he meant. Well, everyone except maybe Jombo, whose notes were colorful and scattered with scrawled drawings, including a pretty decent facsimile of Jorg in stick shape.

"Tira," Sonsil focused on me, and I sat forward instead of melting into the chair like usual. "You'll be our scout. Go in, avoid detection, and report back how many traps or guards they have. Do not engage unless absolutely necessary."

Well, those were different words. Usually it was "retreat and report." I guess Sonsil really wanted to make sure we retrieved Jorg in one piece. He was telling me that I could engage if it meant the difference between saving or losing him, and I nodded my understanding.

"Rachel, you will be in the control van, blocking outgoing comms. If they have networks, I want them tracked. If they try to call their mom, I want to know about it."

Rachel nodded, though I sensed her tense up. She wanted to go into the heart of the action. But her explosive powers were dangerous, especially in close quarters like these. Best to keep her in a safer spot for everyone involved. Besides, her training on the ship where she'd grown up included the ability to hack into port security to sneak in undetected, since they'd had a few Traded on board.

That had come in handy. And made it damn clear why she'd been recruited into the Guild.

Unlike others.

"Gorsel," Sonsil said, with perfect timing. "You'll cover the rear entrance, but here," he brought up a building across the street. "Stay out of sight," meaning he'd be a rock, "and intervene only if Tira runs into trouble." He nodded, closing his fists. Gorsel didn't mind basically being my extraction team. He could take hits easily, pick me up when I was drugged up, and break down doors if they happened to be in the way.

Like a Traded battering ram. Guess I could see why I'd been partnered up with him. Since I was usually the scout, my chances of needing extraction were usually pretty high. Although, of all the missions I'd been on over the past few weeks since I'd become a full operative, I'd rarely needed extraction. But every time I had, it had been pretty memorable.

Maybe I should send Gorsel a thank you card or something.

"Jombo," the large lizard man sat up, his tail shifting excitedly behind him, moving the whole row of seats. Jombo did not have the same tail reservations that I did. I envied him that and found it extremely annoying all at once. "You're on watch duty here," the other side of the building came up.

"Lori and Jackie," he addressed the other two operatives, who had the supremely cool ability of flight. Lori, with weird shimmering wings that by all rights were too small to support her body, and Jackie through some kind of very focalized energy displacement. She could lift nothing else but herself. It was no surprise when Sonsil indicated they'd be air support and selected two nearby buildings as their scouting positions.

Lori looked like a fairy with her tiny wings and

equally shimmery hair, and Jackie just kind of looked like a super model with black flowing hair and dark skin. I really wanted to be their friend, but I was way too intimidated.

Sonsil paused and looked at each of us in turn, his hands behind his back. "This mission is classified as for training purposes," he said softly, "and it would be wise not to tell others of this assignment. You've all been selected for your skills, but also your ability to stay the course and be discreet. There are greater forces at play, and not being detected during this mission is crucial." Was he focusing on me more than the others? "Be safe, be aware, and be quiet."

He curtly nodded and the image vanished from the screen as he stepped out of the room without another word.

I jumped up, eager to get going and follow the first solid lead on Ian.

Please let this be over, soon.

6

RACHEL STOPPED the van on a side street near the convenience store—close enough to catch even short-range transmissions, but not so close as to make people go "hey, that van looks like it's spying on that store."

I stood up as she joined me in the back, activating her scanning equipment. I double-checked my own gear. I only carried a sword and two guns—oh, and a knife, too. And darts. I grinned at Rachel, my hand on the door handle. "See you soon."

"Be careful," Rachel said. She looked like she wanted to say more but couldn't quite get it out and instead she turned back to the screens. In the dark of night, my shadows quickly came to me and I slipped out of the van, closing the door behind me.

Not a soul wandered the street, not too surprising this late at night. The ambassador's reception had ended just five hours ago, and my stomach churned as I drew on my powers yet again.

I ignored it and carefully walked toward the convenience store. The strength of my shadows had often been tested and I knew I could trust them. But I also knew that they weren't foolproof. Infrared, for example, would betray my presence. Some other Traded had the power to see past my shadows. Heck, the right scanning device would find my earpiece, which kept me connected to the team. Even my own breath could betray me if I wasn't careful in the chilly night air.

My guild taught me to be aware of what exactly I should be afraid of. That was the first step to being safer, I suppose.

Nobody said anything on the comms channel. They wouldn't unless it proved necessary, which was a comforting thought. Silence meant no immediate threat.

I skirted the back of the convenience store.

Pulling my shadows more tightly around me, I reached for the door. It was locked, which wasn't surprising. I quickly picked the simple five-pin deadbolt, pushed the door opened, and winced at the terrible creak. I slipped into the dark hallway before someone came to check. Next mission, I'd oil the damn hinges before opening a door.

Navigating the darkness wasn't an issue, since I had my shadows to guide me. I just hoped that no traps waited for me as I quietly made my way toward the front, first, to clear it. The place smelled of old hot dogs, turning my stomach. I ignored it and cleared each aisle, to make sure nothing would come up behind me. Something sticky got on my shoe (gross). Now I squeaked with every step.

Great.

I grabbed some wet wipes from a shelf, keeping the shadows around me, and cleaned under my shoe. It was a risk, because unless I wrapped my shadows really tightly around me when in tight quarters like this, bits of the shelves would vanish within my shadows. But it was a necessary risk.

I placed the wipes back on the shelf and continued my silent tour, clearing an office, a storeroom, and a small and surprisingly clean bathroom.

The only space left was the basement. I listened carefully, but nothing caught my ear. No word from my team on my earpiece. Good. That meant everything was just as quiet out there.

The basement door was suspiciously new. Everything else in the vicinity looked scuffed and old, but this thing was downright shiny. And thick, too. Probably something blast proof.

And, of course, it had a digital combo lock on it. My picks wouldn't be of any use here. I activated my gauntlet tablet (which I affectionately called gaublet, though that hadn't caught on at the guild) and brought it near the lock, tapping for Rachel to take control and pick this sucker for me.

Gaublet could do it, but the poor thing was much slower than Rachel, so it could just enjoy the show. Rachel didn't disappoint, the door gently popping open.

Be careful flashed across the screen before it darkened again.

Taking the warning to heart, I waited a few heartbeats before slipping in, just in case someone intended to send a volley of bullets my way. With enough concentration, I could actually push my shadows to stop others, but they were no match for fast-moving bullets.

Slight orange light brightened my path down the stairs. I pulled out my handgun/taser combo (loved that thing), just in case. Each step proved terrifying as I kept an eye out for tripwires or traps, but nothing exploded.

I cleared the stairs, turned the corner, and stepped into the basement. The whole of it, as far as I could tell. Old coolers had been pushed aside to make way for new equipment. Shelves lined with beakers and vials. Computer screens, though the hard drives all seemed to be gone. And a stench I recognized all too easily.

In the center of the room, strapped down on a metal table, lay Jorg Loops.

What remained of him, anyway. We were too late.

7

AFTER HAVING CLEARED THE ROOM, Sonsil slipped in, Dame Zallir close on his heels. They both looked like they'd eaten some particularly nasty sauerkraut, too. I dropped my shadows, since I doubted they'd like feeling like I was trying to eavesdrop on them.

Rachel and Lori were next, with their cool evidence kits in hand, to see if any traces had been left behind.

"Clear this area and see if you can figure out anything that'll lead us to who did this," Sonsil said. Dame Zallir observed Jorg's mutilated body. They'd cut out his teeth, leaving a bloody grin behind.

I'd much preferred the toothy one from his picture.

She scowled and gave Sonsil a dark look before storming back up the stairs. I guess we weren't so worried about being detected anymore.

Sonsil stepped to the side, away from where Rachel and Lori had started working. He crossed his arms, glanced toward the table, looking grim. He didn't exactly invite conversation, but I couldn't help it. I had to know.

"Do we know if he was taken by the same people who took Ian?" I whispered.

"We do," Sonsil said, his voice equally low, but traveling to every corner of the room, stuffing it with the unspoken words.

"Do you think he's...did they," I couldn't quite put my fears into words. "...to Ian?"

"No," Sonsil said with such certainty that I couldn't help but believe him. "Until we find him, we assume he's alive. Understood?"

I nodded, and he turned and vanished up the stairs. Rachel observed me for a few seconds before focusing back on her work, trying to figure something out with a modem.

Jorg's body made my stomach turn even more, but I tried to observe as closely as possible. To detect any clue that might help me find Ian. Forcing my stomach to stay calm, I approached the body.

They hadn't just cut out his teeth. He was missing one of his arms. I tried to focus on the wounds to see what kind of cuts they were, but I had to glance down, heart in my throat.

What little there was in my stomach would end up on their clean floor soon...*wait*. Clean floor? With a missing limb, there should be a hell of a lot of blood.

Unless they'd taken it, first. My breath caught in my throat, pushing the threatening lump out. When I'd first met Ian, he'd been trapped in a room full of animals. Animals with missing body parts. And we'd retrieved a canister from whoever had done that. A canister apparently full of *something* from the animals. Or so we'd thought.

I glanced around for a similar canister, but there wasn't anything like that around. Not that I'd expect it. They'd have taken that away when they'd abandoned their facility.

Who were they?

They were the ones who'd hired Glitter to infiltrate guilds. The ones who'd created chaos and distraction, killing multiple Traded in a bid to get the few who were different. Like, different even for Traded. Those who had come before the one great swap from twenty years ago. Those who had arrived on earth without the price the rest of humanity had to pay when we arrived: losing a human baby, traded with a baby from another world.

The different Traded, who were older. Who remembered their home planets. Who'd arrived here for reasons that were as unknown as the reason for the giant swap that followed.

And then…nothing. No more Traded. A trickle, a boom, and an end.

Or was it? Had there been others after us? I didn't know, and I doubted anyone would have told us. Hell, they barely told us anything about this world, trying to insulate us, to keep us focused on a single purpose and guild.

No matter how much I casually looked around while playing security for Rachel and Lori, I couldn't see anything else of importance. I didn't know anything about science, so I couldn't tell what the beakers and glass stuff were for. I didn't know enough about tech to guess what kind of installation they'd ripped out.

I'd have to wait for Lori and Rachel's report. Lori was now pouring over the body, preparing it for transport to a guild for further analysis. Not our guild. We didn't do that part. We'd leave here, and someone else would come claim it.

The guilds were insular enough that we couldn't swap information with others. We couldn't build networks with other Traded to learn more about our role. Our purpose.

If there was any.

"We're done," Lori said, her singsong voice out of place as she ripped off her gore-covered gloves. My stomach flip-flopped and I nodded, wrapping my shadows around all three of us as we walked up the stairs. We headed back to the Guild of Shadows to wait until the next mission called, hoping it wouldn't lead us to Ian's body.

8

LAYERS OF LEAVES, vines and rocks lent Ian's room a cavernous vibe. Of course, he had an actual cavern made of rocks, which he liked to sleep in, so that helped the whole atmosphere. The special lights shone softer at times, brighter at others, set on a timer to promote growth.

Or something like that.

I didn't know much, but I was pretty sure plants needed some form of sun to survive, and we didn't exactly get windows at the Guild of Shadows. Sonsil had seen to it that Ian's plants were moved from the satellite branch of the Guild to the main one, and I'd tried to integrate them.

Most had survived, so I couldn't be doing that bad. Mist flew from the spray bottle, forming dew on leaves as I tended to the plants the way I'd seen Ian do for months. While we chatted about this and that, or just sat in friendly silence.

It wasn't perfect, our friendship. But he'd been there

when I'd needed him. And he'd been kind to me, which was rare.

Plus, Ian didn't fit in. Like me. He was awkward, like he always wanted to be in a different shape than human. A dog, a raccoon, a snail, even…anything but the bipedal creature that needed to stand at the front of rooms and talk to people.

It took me the longest time to figure out why Sonsil had selected him as his second-in-command. At first, I thought it was because Ian seemed kind of like a son to Sonsil. But that would be mean, since Ian didn't seem to enjoy the position, despite being good at it. Then, once I'd learned he was an older Traded, I thought it was because of that. More knowledge of his powers, and he'd grown up in the budding Guild of Shadows.

But now, after weeks of him being absent, I was pretty sure I actually understood why. It was because we could see ourselves in Ian. He could *look* human, sure, but he never looked like he fit in. His skin was uncomfortable. And he'd chosen to be kind, instead of taking his angst out on the world. Two traits that made the Traded comfortable around him, and also made us care for him.

The door opened and I whipped around, surprised to find Rachel there. She looked just as shocked to see me, then gave an awkward laugh that would have made Ian proud.

"I should have known you'd be here," she said.

"I'm trying to keep these alive," I pointed to the plants.

"That's what I was coming to do, too," she grinned, then made up her mind and stepped into the room.

"Oh," I said, surprised not to be the only one who'd thought of taking care of Ian's plants.

"I didn't even know he had all of these back in the old Guild," Rachel said, looking around at the green foliage. Well, most of it was green. "I helped move them, and then just wanted to do a little something to help Ian out."

I nodded, feeling better that she hadn't known about his plants. Ian was such a private person, and he'd shared his secret with me. Re-affirming that the connection we'd shared was special and private made me feel better.

"So Sonsil thinks Jorg was related to Ian's kidnapping," Rachel blurted out.

"Rachel," I said, looking at her with wide eyes and automatically checking around to make sure we weren't being listened to. "We're not supposed to talk about that."

"It's not bugged," she crossed her arms. "I checked before. And why shouldn't we talk about it? Why shouldn't we try to save an operative of the Guild? Why couldn't we try to save our friend, Tira?"

Rachel seemed to use the word friend a lot more freely than I did, and maybe I could learn something from her. But Rachel wasn't just in it to save Ian, and I knew that.

"You want to avenge your crew," I said softly. Her entire crew, slaughtered by one of their own, taken over by Glitter's mind-altering powers.

"I do, but I also want to save our friend. I don't see why the two have to be mutually exclusive."

"I guess they don't," I agreed, then shook my head. "Sonsil told me that if anyone was caught looking for Ian, they'd be declared rogue."

"I don't understand why we can't look for him!" Rachel threw her hands up in disgust. "Are we supposed to just follow a trail of bodies until it leads to his?"

Her eyes widened and she looked like she regretted her words. I held up my hand to stop her apology. "No, you're right," I sighed. "I just have a hard time getting others involved when it could get them hurt, you know?"

She grinned. "That's what makes you a good friend."

While I stood there, stunned at just how freely she used the word friend, she pulled out her laptop from her bag and sat down on a rock, indicating I should do the same.

"This is what I've got so far," she said, "and don't worry, this one isn't traceable, even by the Guild. I made sure." She tapped a skull and crossbones icon at the bottom of her screen. Seeing my blank look, she rolled her eyes. "It's a massive security blocker. I created it with a few others back when I used to sail."

She trailed off, then rallied herself. "Okay, so, I have three other names of Traded who were taken at the same time as Ian. And it took me that long to find them," she said, names and pictures popping up.

Lorna, from the Wolf Pack League, who was probably an agent for the Guild of Shadows, was first up on the list. Her, I knew. Hell, I'd been there during the attack that had seen her disappear.

A boy named Ni'inch, wearing an orange turban and a serious expression, and fairly human looking.

And a girl named Malarky, with a head much too elongated to be human. That, and five sets of eyes.

The list included Jorg, too, but he was now crossed off.

And Ian.

Five, all together.

"It's not much," she said, "but guilds aren't big on sharing information. I've had to hack my way around and mostly intercept communiques to figure that much out. I don't think Sonsil even knows. It's like they don't want to acknowledge that they were taken at all. And I'm still not sure why they were targeted."

I glanced sideways at Rachel, then sighed. There was no point holding back anymore. I'd have to respect her choice to assume the risk.

"He didn't come to earth twenty-one years ago," I said, feeling like I was betraying his confidence. Rachel looked at me with wide eyes, but waited for me to continue. "He came a few years earlier, and remembers some of his home world. I know Lorna did, too. They're different than us. An earlier generation of Traded, or something. Not part of the big swap."

Rachel looked from me to the pictures on her laptop, assimilating the information. "That's…I had no idea," she whispered.

"Me, neither. And I don't think we're really supposed to know."

"Of course not," Rachel sneered. "The less we know, the easier it is to keep us under control." She took a moment to compose herself, her skin tone changing slightly. If she lost too much control, she'd explode. Literally. And blow up the room and all of Ian's plants.

"Why would Glitter be gathering them?"

For a split second, I hesitated. Like saying it out loud made it more real.

"They're harvesting something from them," I said, stomach turning again at the thought of Ian's blood being drained. "I know blood. There was no blood at that scene, despite an arm being cut off. And Jorg's teeth were gone, too."

Rachel's face twisted for a half-second before she frowned and brought up his file.

"His right arm could fire lasers," Rachel said. "Not, like, damaging ones. Just showy ones. He was in the circus guild, basically as a super-targeted spotlight."

"Poor guy."

"Yeah. And his teeth were fangs. Tira," she turned to me, wide-eyed, "what if they're harvesting the body parts that make them Traded? What if they're looking for something in the things that are most different about us?"

A chill crawled up my spine.

"Ian..."

"He's a shifter," Rachel followed my thoughts, mumbling, "so all of him is powered up, if you will. They might go for bone marrow, or spinal fluids..."

I stood up abruptly, not wanting to hear more. Rachel put down her laptop, face set with determination. "I'm sorry! I didn't mean to sound so callous. But that's not a bad thing, Tira. Unlike an arm, those regenerate. They might keep him alive longer to harvest more from him!"

"I think I'm going to be sick," I mumbled, trying to find fresh air, sticking my head near the cave and its framing foliage.

"I think we can save him," Rachel said, bringing her knees up to her chest. "I failed to save one crew, Tira. I swear I won't fail this one, too."

My stomach twisted with grief for Rachel. "You didn't fail anyone," I said between deep breaths. "And you'll never fail us either, Rachel. This world though. It's a bitch."

She was silent for a few seconds, then laughter bubbled out of her even as tears escaped her eyes. "This world *is* a bitch," she said, erupting with more laughter. I let it run its course, while I fought to regain control of my stomach. Eventually, we both evened out and I sat back down beside her.

"So, what do we do next?" I asked, feeling better for having an ally. Someone else cared, and saving Ian wasn't all on me.

"Next," she said, grinning at me, "I take your information and see if I can find Glitter."

"Start here," I grinned back, handing her a folded piece of paper with dates and GPS coordinates. "All incidents that could link up to Glitter. Of people losing their minds, or doing stuff really out of the ordinary. Enough to get a mention."

"Sounds good," she took the piece of paper and

folded it up in her shirt. "I promise I won't let anyone see this."

"Thanks," I said, standing back up. "Well, I'd better get back to my quarters and get some sleep. It's been a while." I hadn't really slept since yesterday, and I was starting to feel it.

"It has," Rachel said. "They've been running you ragged."

"No more than anyone else," I shrugged. Rachel gave me a look that told me I didn't quite seem to understand the situation, but she didn't pursue it. "Anyway, I can sleep most of the day away, so we can chat when the sun sets?"

"Sounds like a plan," she said, then looked me in the eye. "I want to find him too, and I'm not the only one. He was kind to me," her voice dropped. "He helped me focus and control my powers better. It's made a world of difference for me."

Without another word, she slipped out of the room.

A few moments passed by before I turned around and finished watering the plants, hoping I was doing more good than harm.

"We'll find him," I promised them, before dragging my tired feet toward my bed.

According to the time, which displayed on the clock by my bed when I slammed it, I slept exactly three hours and fourteen minutes before the knock at my door woke me up. I managed to stumble out of bed and open the door, ready to chew out whoever was bothering me.

Until I saw that it was Dame Zallir standing there.

"Oh," I said. She raised an eyebrow, and I wiped my face with my pajama sleeve, trying to look like I hadn't just rolled out of bed.

A battle I highly doubted I was winning.

"Sorry to disturb you," she said. I scoffed in disbelief, then tried to hide it with a cough. I choked instead. By the time I'd regained my composure (about a thousand years later), Dame Zallir still looked perfectly calm, like she merely waited for the bus to show up.

I was pretty sure I was bright purple from all the coughing.

"Dame Zallir," I managed to squeak out, which threatened to make me cough again.

"I just wanted to alert you that you are being deployed before sunrise, in three hours," she said. I nodded, though that was odd. Usually we were brought into mission rooms for debriefs. Instead, she handed me a file. A paper file.

I'd never received one of those at the Guild of Shadows.

"Um, thank you," I said, glad my voice was holding out, even though I sounded like I'd swallowed a gerbil.

"You are to tell no one of this, and familiarize yourself with the contents before disposing of the file."

"Okay," I said, flipping the file open. It just had one picture. The ambassador's daughter, whose life I'd saved. She looked younger and held a baby wrapped in her arms.

"I didn't know she had a baby," I said.

"She doesn't, anymore," Dame Zallir said, her voice low. "That picture was taken more than twenty years ago."

"Ok," I said. So she had a grown daughter. Maybe I'd need to protect her, too. Or, the Guild was slipping and this was the best picture they had.

"You're to protect her and stay by her side," Dame Zallir continued.

"The ambassador's daughter, or the baby...I mean, daughter? ...his granddaughter?"

A choking fit would be very welcome right now. But no such luck. I looked up to Dame Zallir, and she studied me with her dark eyes, as though trying to figure out just how much of an idiot I was. Current evidence indicated that I was a fairly big one, and should just be left alone to sleep the week away.

"His daughter," she thankfully broke the silence. "And there's the report on the attack." Instead of handing me a paper file, gaublet vibrated on my nightstand, indicating a new upload.

"Review the files, and be ready to leave in three hours," I thought she would turn to go, but something seemed to keep her here. If I were her, I'd be reevaluating sending me to protect this woman. Unless she wanted her dead, of course.

"Just…pay attention, Tira. Use your head. And speak to no one about this mission. I mean it, Tira. No one."

"Got it," I said. She examined me another moment, then turned on her heel and vanished down the corridor. Yawning, I turned back to my room to review the files so I could get a few more hours of sleep.

I sat in bed and read the files uploaded to gaublet. It wasn't much, really. Details on the attack. I couldn't spot anything super weird, which only seemed to amplify Dame Zallir's words to pay attention and use my head. Either she thought I was an idiot (which, fair, but I wasn't my best when just waking up), or she really needed me to see something.

But what? A hint would be okay, but that didn't seem likely.

A schematic of the centipede thing I'd destroyed with a cryo pellet flashed on gaublet. Full analysis followed its dissection. Robotic, except for the acid it spit out. *No shit.* I still felt the sting of having lost my favorite shirt. I glanced over the details, and a red tag caught my attention.

Substance unknown. Organic. From Traded?

A chill ran down my spine. I couldn't figure out if I was just freaking myself out after seeing the gore in that basement, but my mind immediately linked the two. Pieces of Traded. Re-utilized in different ways.

I wish I'd have kept a copy of Rachel's files. Maybe one of the other missing Traded had some kind of acid ability? Maybe…maybe they'd harvested them?

No. It couldn't be. Could it?

Show no one.

Dame Zallir's words still rang in my ear, but the sight of Jorg's toothless grin more so. Ian was running out of time. And, if there was any connection to him, no matter how tenuous, I had to pursue it.

I grabbed some paper and painstakingly made a copy, leaving it on my desk for Rachel to find. She'd come to meet me in the morning and I'd be gone, but I'd leave her a message. She was smart and resourceful. She'd know not to leave a trail.

And she'd see something in there I'd probably missed, which hopefully would lead us to Ian.

10

I STOOD in the same centipede room, except the floor had been fixed and a nice rug added to cover whatever damage lay beneath. I hid in my shadows, and tried not to yawn. Nightmares had invaded what little sleep I'd managed to finally claim last night. Ian strapped to a table. Ian being torn apart. Ian's blood in a centipede. Ian asking me why I hadn't saved him.

I really needed some nighttime meditation routine. I used to talk to Ian about my fears. To mouse Ian, or sometimes raccoon Ian. Or my favorite: puppy Ian (aka Max). It was easier, somehow, talking to someone who looked super cute and just listened. That you could cuddle with, and not be awkward with arms. Not having him around robbed me of an outlet I didn't realize I'd come to rely on.

The ambassador's daughter walked into the room, and I held my breath. Partly because of how fabulous she looked in a long, bright pink and gold-trimmed dress. Partly because I really hoped she didn't realize I was here.

"Would you show yourself to me?"

Damn it. Not my lucky day.

"Um, I'd prefer not to." To her credit, she didn't jump.

"Alright, then," she sounded disappointed. I just felt relieved. Then she ruined that, too.

"Can we talk?"

I shifted my feet. She glanced toward me but averted her glance, as though realizing it made me uncomfortable, and headed to focus on the papers covering her large, dark desk. She seemed kind. I liked that.

"I'm supposed to keep an eye out to keep you safe," I mumbled, wishing I could project my voice so she couldn't home in on me so easily. She kept her hands busy shuffling papers. Like she tried to force herself not to look.

Her head slowly lowered, the sun caressing her dark braids. I stood rooted in place, fascinated by her graceful movements. The hint of something earthy, her perfume, maybe, struck me. Unlike most human scents, this one proved pleasing.

"I understand," she said, then sighed, like her entire body deflated. Then it quickly reinflated as she stood straight, like a beacon. "I just...I'd love to get a few answers. Your people are harder to find than you'd believe."

"I don't have a people," I said, though I couldn't help

but wonder if she meant my planet. Maybe she knew something about my home world that I didn't.

Another long pause. "Not here, I suppose. I meant Traded. My apologies."

I was grateful when a tall, slick-haired man walked into the room.

"We need to talk," he said. I didn't like the rough sound of his voice.

"No, we don't, Job," she turned her back to him, and he took a threatening step toward her. I didn't hesitate to stop him. My job was to protect her, and the guy seemed pretty sketchy. Except she seemed to know him, so maybe a gentle approach would be best.

I threw a sleeping dart. His hand went up to his neck, but before he could reach it, he tumbled and fell forward.

She turned around, surprised, taking in his form sprawled on the ground. Her eyes grew wide but she didn't move, as if too shocked to speak. Then a large snore erupted from him.

She broke down laughing.

"That's wonderful," she said, once she'd regained her composure. "But, just to be clear, I don't actually need protection from him. He's more annoying than dangerous."

"Oh. Okay."

She focused on my voice and hesitated for one second before convincing herself to keep moving forward.

"I get that you don't want me to see you, and I

respect that. Would you be willing to let me know your name?"

"Um, why?"

"So I can address you with it. It seems more polite."

Perhaps because of a lack of imagination, I couldn't think of a reason not to.

"Tira Misu." I waited for her mouth to do that thing humans do, when they realized a demon girl had been named after a dessert. With the (rather foolish) hopes that she'd become sweet.

Except she simply nodded, and smiled. "It's lovely to meet you, Tira. I'm Aia Ecsuda. You can just call me Aia." Then, even more kindly, she turned her back, called someone in, and explained to them that he'd collapsed. Paramedics took him away, but not before I'd retrieved the dart.

She still seemed amused when they were gone. I feared she'd try to start up a conversation, but she sat down at her desk instead and started reviewing notes on her digital pad.

The rest of the day proved boring, though I was pretty proud of how easily I kept my shadows wrapped around me. As much as I hated to admit it, it showed that I was comfortable here. Despite what they believed, that pushing us to the brink helped our powers grow (which, granted, had worked a few times for me), I found mine easiest to control when I wasn't riddled with anxiety.

And, right now, I really wasn't. There were no known threats, everything was super quiet, and I was bored out of my mind. She even left me a plate of food while she worked in the evening. That was pretty nice, with flat breads and a variety of tasty dips.

My mind started to wander back to the puzzle of Ian, Jorg, Lorna, and the other missing Traded. But a lump formed in my throat, making my shadows harder to control. So I tried my best to return my focus to the nothing happening around me.

I wished I'd have asked Dame Zallir extra questions. Like, how long I was supposed to shadow Aia. I certainly wasn't about to abandon my post without some clarification. The Guild of Shadows hated failed missions.

Without any word from them by bedtime, I followed Aia up to her room, surprised to see blankets out on a cot near her bed.

"My father won't let me be without security," she said, speaking to the room as if I was standing there. I shifted so she was sort of addressing me, finding comfort in the semi-darkness, only a candle (an actual candle!) lighting the room. It was a large space with an enormous bed, a sitting area and elaborate furniture. "But that doesn't mean you shouldn't get some rest."

I sighed and slipped into the darkness cast by the tall dresser, dropping my shadows. I could stay awake for a while if necessary, but holding up my shadows for so long had proven exhausting. And I'd barely slept the night before, so some sleep would be good for me.

I wasn't sure Dame Zallir would see it that way, however.

"I'm still not sure what I'm protecting you from," I

said softly. She turned, her eyes betraying her surprise at seeing me there, even though I was mostly wrapped in the room's darkness. Not that it mattered. I mean, she'd seen me already and hadn't screamed. But I'd been pretty drugged up then, so I hadn't really cared.

Now, I cared.

She barely missed a beat.

"Whoever has been trying to assassinate my father," she said, sitting down on the edge of the bed. She hesitated, chewing on her lower lip until she seemed to catch herself, and whispered. "You don't have to hide from me."

With a slight gesture, she indicated the cot near the end of her bed. It did look comfortable, and I'd been standing all day.

She's already seen you, Tira!

Those words didn't comfort me as much as I'd hoped, but I took a deep breath and stepped into the room, closer to the dim light of the flame.

"I'm used to humans screaming at me," I shrugged, damned aware that my tail twitched twice with nerves. I sat on it to keep it in place, though it twinged my lower back.

"I promise I won't," she said. I examined her for a few moments. I liked how the flame flickered patterns on her perfect skin, dark like the night. She seemed to be trying hard not to reach out and touch me, even her eyes misting over a bit.

I decided it was time to switch subjects. "Do you have any idea who tried to kill your father, or why?"

She looked surprised. "You...you really don't know

who my father is?"

I shrugged. "They don't exactly keep us abreast of human politics."

"I suppose not," she mumbled, though she looked perturbed again. "My father is Ambassador Tyrese. He's leading the global movement for Traded Integration."

She stopped, eyes narrowing slightly as though gauging my reaction.

"Okay," I said simply. I had no clue what she meant, and it didn't matter. I was integrated into the Guild of Shadows already. That was done.

"Do you know what that means?" she asked softly.

I shrugged. "I don't think I have the right contextual tools to even guess."

She took a deep, shaky breath. "It means we're trying to free you. To let you actually be a part of human society."

"Oh."

"Oh?"

"I mean, I've seen human society." A pause. "Humans are the ones who decided what happens to us, remember?"

She released her breath, slowly. "I do," she seemed to fold in on herself, like guilt weighed her down and she couldn't bear to look at me. Then her back straightened and she gazed out the window, toward the moon, as though it revealed something to her that I couldn't see. "Our own people were enslaved, once, long ago, by other humans, too."

Figured.

"We tried to stop the Traded movement, and have succeeded in some countries…but so many of you are still trapped."

"For countries?" I repeated slowly. "Like, entire countries where Traded roam free?" Skepticism and awe struggled for dominance in my voice.

"Yes," her smile seemed genuine. "And it'll happen here, too. If we're not killed."

"Why is the Guild of Shadows helping you?"

"The what?" she asked. Her turn to be confused. Well, at least she was in good company. I guess I probably shouldn't go around talking to humans and mention the guild name. The line that separated guilds from other guilds seemed to extend to humans, too. Then why was I here? Who the hell had hired us out?

Before either of us could ask another question, gaublet gently vibrated. Not enough to even make a sound, but enough for me to know that a message from the Guild of Shadows had come in.

I looked down at my bracer, struck it twice to activate the screen.

A message from Rachel. The blood drained out of my head.

They found Ni'inch's body.

"What is it?" Aia asked, concerned. I shut down my screen, barely able to breathe.

"You should get some rest," I said softly, wrapping the shadows around me as I stood, putting a clear end to our conversation.

Ni'inch. One of the five names on my list in Ian's room.

Taken at the same time as Ian, by the same people. And his body had just turned up.

11

Tira.

Ian. He was calling for me, but I couldn't reach him. Ripped out of my grasp, taken right in front of me while I struggled to move, still under Glitter's spell.

Tira.

Ian! Hang on! If I could just shake free of Glitter's control, I could reach him in time…

"Tira." I jerked awake, dagger in hand. Aia knelt beside me, not backing away from the demon girl now holding a dagger, to her credit.

"You were having a bad dream," she whispered. I squinted, dawn piercing through the window. I'd fallen asleep even though I hadn't meant to, sitting in the corner formed by the dresser and the wall.

"Sorry," I mumbled, struggling to shove the remaining threads of the nightmare away while I sheathed my knife. Eviscerating the client probably wouldn't make the Guild super happy.

"Are you alright?" she asked so softly that I flushed, embarrassed.

"I'm fine," I said, standing up slowly, stretching my back. She stood as well. She looked like she wanted to reach out to me, but decided against it.

"Sorry to have bothered you."

"You were no bother," she said so softly I almost didn't hear. Then she pulled herself back together. "Do you like eggs and bacon?"

"That sounds delicious." I was damn hungry, and chances were I'd have to keep my shadows up for another entire day. Lots of protein would help me maintain energy. I glanced down at gaublet, quickly checking for any messages that I'd missed while I'd slept unheroically on my watch.

Have lead. Will report back.

Damn it, Rachel. She shouldn't be going off alone. With any luck, she'd have taken Jombo with her. Except I knew that she wouldn't have, because Jombo didn't know anything.

A large plate of food soon appeared in the sitting area, and Aia shooed away the server while I stayed hidden in the bedroom. If I tried to summon my shadows now, I was pretty sure I'd just get a thin sheen. If I were lucky.

"I'll get changed," she said and gracefully vanished into the washroom while I gaped at the amount of food. Piles of bacon, and sausages, and fried eggs. And a tower of toast, for me! Plus, some fruit I'd never tried. And coffee! Okay, I hated coffee. But I still drank it, grateful for a shot of caffeine. Much better than Tradenaline.

Once I was very, very full, I did a few stretches and cleaned up in the powder room, then waited for Aia to re-emerge. She took my breath away when she did. Dark hair flowing, red dress over loose slacks, fetching high heels, silver and gold jewelry. Not too much, not too little. She knew how to get attention.

She looked like she wanted to ask me something. I resisted the urge to vanish, but then she simply nodded and headed for the door. I called my shadows to me and fell in step beside her, hoping I'd get to dart someone else.

That would help me relax.

1 2

THE DAY PASSED WITHOUT INCIDENT. I tried hard to stifle yawns and didn't always succeed, though Aia didn't say anything. She focused on work, with no visitors to interrupt her. She'd probably planned that second part, to stop me from having any fun.

Guard duty was boring. I didn't know how anyone —in the history of time, on any planet— managed to stay focused while keeping watch when absolutely nothing was going on. Was I really needed here? I could be looking for Ian!

Pay close attention, Dame Zallir had said. *Use your head.* Well, okay. I wasn't really doing either of those things right now, but those weren't super clear instructions, either. Pay close attention to what?

I glanced to Aia, who sat at her large desk, looking down at her tablet and pushing documents to her secondary stationary screen. She wore fetching gold reading glasses, now, too. Maybe Dame Zallir hadn't meant to pay close attention for potential attacks.

Shit. I was supposed to spy on Aia, wasn't I? Aia, who'd been kind to me. Aia, who'd given me a huge breakfast and a cot that I'm sure would have been super comfy had I used it.

I hated myself for it, but my allegiance had to be to the Guild of Shadows. The thought of Blake having the controlling tattoo codes made my fingers numb. Was that the price of failure? To be handed over to the Watch?

I held my shadows tightly around me and crept forward, slowly rounding the corner, careful not to reveal my presence as I moved behind her. She seemed none the wiser as she looked over some documents with dense, tiny text. No wonder she needed glasses.

Glancing at the desk didn't help much. There were papers everywhere, and I couldn't exactly rifle through them. I scanned them carefully until my eyes caught the corner of a photo peeking out from beneath some files. Enough for me to recognize who it was.

Lorna. The old woman from the Wolf Pack League who'd been taken by the same people as Ian. *Why does she have a picture of her?*

I debated asking her, when I noticed the wall on her left was buckling and red, a scorch mark spreading from the center like tendrils. Without thinking, I grabbed Aia and pulled her away in one swift motion, throwing us both behind the couch. An instant later, the wall exploded outward, sending the couch and us flying back.

"Stay quiet and move quickly with me," I whispered to Aia as I wrapped my shadows around us both. She nodded, eyes set. We both stood up and I pushed her in to the adjoining parlor. It was filled with rich velvet couches, two fireplaces, and more ostentatious portraits than I cared to count. I didn't have time to appreciate the finery, feeling the heat build behind me as the wall surrounding the door frame caught fire.

Several security guards rushed in carrying extinguishers, not realizing the fire wasn't their biggest problem.

"Get out of there," I shouted at them, but it was too late. Three of them went flying back as a blast caught them in the chest.

Shit. I'd compromised our position for no good reason.

Humans.

The ground buckled, throwing us to our knees. My shadows danced angrily around me, my hand clasping Aia's wrist for fear she'd freak out and run out of my shadows.

A figure stepped through the flaming door frame, blue eyes glowing, pink hair matted with blood, and blue skin shimmering with power.

It took half a second for me to process what I was looking at. Somehow, I managed not to gasp.

Rachel. Full decked-out power Rachel, apparently intent on killing the person I was supposed to protect.

I ran through possibilities as I held Aia in place, too worried I'd give our position away with a creaking floorboard. Rachel slowly scanned the room with her disturbing eyes. I'd never seen her so brimming with power. She barely looked like herself.

Could the Guild have sent someone to attack this place while another member guarded it? I doubted that, but couldn't dismiss it. Was this somehow Blake's doing? Messing with me with his Watch authority? Did Rachel have a Twin? Okay, that one I really doubted.

Her eyes locked on mine for half a second as her gaze swept past me. I recognized the blank look. The fluid actions with vague purpose. The lost gaze.

Glitter. She was under Glitter's control. She *had* to be. Rachel wouldn't do this. And she'd said she was following a lead…

Shit.

My wrist glowed for half a second with an infinity symbol, mark of the Guild of Shadows. Help was on the way. I clicked on gaublet. Two minutes away.

Double shit.

If they took down Rachel, they might kill her, not even realizing what was happening. Especially if they thought she'd just gone rogue.

I was really starting to dislike that word.

I turned to Aia, let her go, and pointed to the doorframe to the left. It was only ten paces away, and I could keep my shadows wrapped around her. Aia nodded, then her eyes grew wide as I pulled out my favorite blade, a thin sword with leather bindings on the handle.

She squeezed my arm as though telling me to be careful, and then slipped away, my shadows keeping her safe.

I focused back on Rachel, who'd started wandering around, narrowing her eyes.

Rachel was strong. Explosively strong. I had to take her out before she even knew I was coming. I slipped my sword back into its scabbard. Cutting her in two wouldn't quite do.

Instead, I pulled a small dart from the Guild emblem on my belt and silently made my way toward her. When I was in range, I flicked my wrist and landed the dart in her glowing arm.

She growled and pulled it out.

She remained standing.

Oh.

From training, I knew that some life forms required more of the sleeping agent, because of science and shit like that. But I'd never encountered one in real life. And I hadn't expected it from one of my own friends.

Rachel stumbled forward, which was great. The poison had had some effect on her. But then she started to glow even more, which was bad.

It meant a massive explosion was coming. I hoped Aia had been smart enough to keep running and warn people away. The Guild would be here any second. And they'd kill Rachel to stop her.

No time to hesitate.

I ran toward her, pulling out my sword again, my shadows falling away in the growing light of Rachel's power. The sleeping agent bought me the time I needed. She didn't spot me right away, her hand coming up just as I leapt over her and struck her with the hilt of my blade, hard. I didn't hold back the blow, even when I noticed the bad wound she'd already suffered. She cried in pain and dropped to her knees.

I landed beside her and grabbed her in a choke hold.

"I'm sorry," I whispered, "but you just need to trust me and let go."

Her neck bulged in anger, her arms scrabbling to try to pull me off, but I held fast, even as my skin began to burn and blister. We raced to see which would go first: her consciousness or her blast. But her powers seemed muted as she struggled against the drugs, and thankfully I won. She finally collapsed, her glow receding as I gently laid her down.

Just then, three more operatives stepped into the room, scanning the destruction before focusing on us —the demon girl with the badly burned arm, and the collapsed operative beside her.

"Hey," I gave them a little wave, only to be rewarded by a grunt from Gorsel.

He really could learn to be a tad more friendly.

"WHERE'S RACHEL?" I demanded of Sonsil as soon as he stepped into my room, where I'd been ungracefully (and ungratefully) thrown in here the moment we'd returned.

"She's getting checked," he said, then relented and added: "she should be fine. We don't disagree with your diagnosis."

That deflated me a bit. I'd had no choice but to mention Glitter, to make sure they wouldn't kill her. But it had also made it pretty damn clear that Rachel had been looking for him, which didn't look good.

"I knew she was looking," I whispered, "but we didn't share information until two nights ago, after we'd found Jorg. She shouldn't pay for my inability to let Ian go."

Sonsil stayed quiet for a moment, hands behind his back. I worked up the courage to glance up into his face.

"Maybe you would have been better to collaborate, Tira," he said softly.

"Anyone who'd have been caught would have been declared rogue. That sounded bad." I kept my own voice low to match the gravity of his tone.

"It is," he said. Another long pause. "But you should consider the value of trusting others. Of the greater strength in numbers, with *trusted* people."

Even I couldn't miss his emphasis.

"Why would Glitter send Rachel after Aia?" I asked, intent on getting any blame deflected from Rachel.

Sonsil's eyebrow shot up. "What makes you think she was after her, Tira?"

I shrugged. "I was told to protect her. And he sent an attack. It makes sense."

The pause proved uncomfortably long.

"It seems to, indeed," he said, then opened the door, indicating I should follow. "But keep an open mind and don't let foregone conclusions cloud your judgment, Tira."

What the hell was that supposed to mean? I had a thousand more questions, but Dame Zallir stepped out from behind Sonsil, giving me a look that basically said "shut up." She was excellent at conveying emotions with her face, that one.

"They're waiting for you," she said softly, her voice less steely than I was used to. Sonsil's jaw tightened a bit.

"Stay here," he said. "It's for your own protection." He closed my door, locking me in.

I still had gaublet, thankfully, and I tapped it

hopefully. Nothing from Rachel. Or anyone. Anything I'd send would be tracked. Still, worth a try…

No luck. Gaublet couldn't pick my door open.

Might as well settle in while the healing salves on my arm finished doing their work.

As I turned to get changed, the door opened again. Blake walked in, looking like he owned the place.

"Hello, demon girl."

1 4

MY TATTOO LIT UP, pain traveling down my neck, through my spine and belly, tingling all the way to my toes and fingers. The last time I'd gone through this—at the Margrave Academy—it would have knocked me out. But I managed to cling to consciousness, though I collapsed to my knees, breathing heavily, trying hard not to scream.

Another jolt from my tattoo, and this time I failed to stay up. I collapsed, cheek cold against the floor.

Boots appeared in my line of sight. Even the way Blake walked was pretentious. I hated him so much. Should have killed him back in school. A bit more murdering might have helped my life in general.

"Why was the embassy attacked twice on *your* watch, Tira Misu?" he said, as though making friendly conversation. I shifted my arms, trying to get feeling back in them, but the tattoo pulsed back to life and my whole body spasmed. If he kept it up, I would pass out.

Like hell he'd get that satisfaction from me.

"Twice, and no other time but when you're there."

"I'm popular," I managed to blurt out, grin on my lips. The tattoo pulsed steadily, but he didn't increase the pain. Instead, he kicked my shoulder and forced me on my back.

My arms flopped uselessly beside me and I stared up at the ceiling, sweat trickling down the sides of my face. My stomach lurched and the room spun.

"Are you jealous I don't have to work at it like you do?" I managed to squeak out. He looked deeply annoyed, but not as angry as I'd hoped. Still, any blow to his ego was good in my books.

"Who are you working with?" he crouched and gently pushed a strand of hair from my face. It took all my willpower not to flinch.

"No one," I whispered. I wouldn't tell him Rachel had been looking for Ian, too. Is that what Sonsil had meant about the consequences of going rogue? That you were left at the Watch's mercy, unable to fight back against the control tattoo? Why had no one stopped him from entering my room?

Blake leaned in, hot breath on my skin, finger tracing the outline of my jaw as he clipped out every word: "I don't believe you."

Pain exploded around my neck and I jerked up, my back arching, a scream trapped within my parted lips, a tunnel of darkness closing over my eyes even as I tried to pull my shadows around me out of pure instinct.

Another jolt from the tattoo knocked the breath out of me and my shadows dropped as my eyes rolled back into my head. I struggled to hold on to a modicum of consciousness. Drifting away seemed like a pleasant idea, especially as I felt Blake's hot breath near my ear, hand possessively on my shoulder.

I hated the tears I felt escape my closed eyes, mingling with the sweat. I hated the feeling of helplessness. Of hopelessness.

Familiar, but after almost a year of reprieve, distant and dim in my mind.

"Remember your place, demon girl," he whispered in my ear. "You are not your own person. You are nothing special. Just another Traded who needs to fall in line. If you don't want to end up like your buddy, Ian."

The mention of Ian's name snapped me back to the present. My hand twitched, anger bringing my limbs back to life.

Without hesitating, I slapped my wrist down and triggered the Tradenaline shot. I shouldn't be taking one so soon, but it would give me speed and counter the pain. The needle stabbed my heart and the jolt shot through my body, my back arching. Blake jerked up in surprised, but too late. I reached for my belt, pulled out another sleeping dart, and jabbed it into the side of his neck.

He grabbed for it and activated the tattoo, but I rolled over him and slammed him down, pinning his hands to his sides. Whatever the hell he did to trigger the tattoo seemed to require his hands, because the pain stopped. I slammed his own gaublet down and smashed it. With any luck, that's where the controls were.

He grinned up at me, though the sleeping dart robbed him of the full strength of his powers. "I'm game if you are, demon girl," he said, narrowing his eyes as he possessively looked at me. Creep. "But I like to be in control."

His powers slammed into me and I couldn't move anymore. I'd been ready for it, though. Unlike Glitter, he couldn't control my body. He could just freeze me in place, and I gripped his wrists so tightly that he couldn't free himself.

"I'll give you reason to scream," he muttered as he tried to get out from under me.

"Me, first," I said, feeling his powers waning as his heart rate increased, the sleeping agent traveling fast through his system. Just like Rachel's powers had been dimmed, so were Blake's. For a second, he looked panicked, realizing he couldn't hold me like he wanted to. Then he smirked, trying damn hard to put on a brave face.

"You really think you can overpower me, demon girl?"

I took a deep breath and managed to lower myself a tiny bit, showing him that he didn't have full control of me. And I squeezed his wrists so tight he yelped and blanched.

"I really do," I said, my voice a creepy whisper, which seemed intentional even though it was just the fact that my throat was ridiculously dry after all that silent screaming, sweating and crying.

"If you hurt me, the Watch will hunt you to the ends of the world."

I ignored him. We were well past the point of idle threats.

"You tell me what you know about Ian," I narrowed my eyes, "or the sleeping agent will knock you out, and then I'll cut my initials in your pretty face, so you'll never forget this day." I leaned in as he swallowed hard, struggling against the drugs. Moving my body was getting easier by the second. "I know I'll forget this almost immediately, but you never will."

His eyes fluttered as he struggled to stay awake.

"I'd talk fast if I were you."

And, to my surprise, he did.

15

I MOVED AS FAST as possible and grabbed a few things, the Tradenaline flowing through my veins, counteracted by the pain of Blake's torture. Wrapping my shadows around me, I put distance between me and bleeding Golden Boy.

I had to get out of there before Blake woke up and slammed his powers into me again. I had to get out of the Guild before they realized what I'd done and locked it down completely to keep me here.

Wiping the fresh blood from my dagger, I sheathed it and stepped out of my room, holding my breath. No one was there.

I didn't know how closely the Guild of Shadows was tied to the Watch, but I knew the power that the Watch held over us. Sonsil would have to hand me in. Even if he wanted to protect me, taking down a Watch agent destroyed my chances of staying here.

Blake's words hastened my steps. *Last I saw him, he*

looked ready to cross death's door. And then he'd passed out.

I reached Rachel's room. I couldn't just leave her behind.

"Rachel?" I whispered. No answer. The door was unlocked, and she wasn't there. My heart leapt into my throat. Where could she be? Maybe the infirmary. Or maybe one of the cells.

Breaking her out would take too much time.

Shit shit shit.

She'd found Glitter. Maybe there was something here that would lead me to him. If I could stop him and find Ian, maybe I could negotiate for her release. Time was running short, and I knew it. Blake would wake up and bring the Watch down on me at any moment.

I'm so sorry, Rachel, I thought as I started rifling through the drawer of her bedside table. There was nothing there, except a few mementos from her crew. I glanced under her mattress. Also empty.

Her room was almost as bare as mine, save for a large picture of the sea. "Reminds me of what's important, and what I love," she'd once confided in me.

Confided in me. Like a friend would do.

I pulled the frame off the wall and looked behind it, but it was blank.

"I'm so sorry, Rachel," I mumbled again, ripping the frame off. My eyes widened. A thin laptop was hidden behind the image. Grabbing one of her bags, I threw it in, then tried to get the frame back together. It was beyond repair. I might have been a bit too rough with it.

"Sorry," I winced as I left it on the ground, hoping it would look like it had fallen off the wall, knowing full well that wouldn't fool anyone.

If she was smart, she'd blame everything on me, the fugitive, and save her skin. Except I knew she wouldn't. She'd never betray her own.

Feeling like the biggest jerk to have ever walked this shitty planet, I slipped out of her room and toward the nearest exit. Gray metallic corridors greeted me until I reached the training rooms, which had more warmth to them, with dark woods and different lighting. Ian and I had slept here a few times, when everything was just too much. Safely, together, in the gentle glow of the night lights.

Regret clutched my chest as I jogged past the rooms, the Tradenaline messing with my breathing. Ian's door came and went, leaving his plants abandoned. There would be no chance to come back and water them, later. I hoped they'd be okay. If they were okay, part of me believed Ian would be okay. Like those plants were part of the legacy he'd left behind, to be tended by me.

Blake had passed out before I could ask more questions. But I knew Ian still lived. That would have to do. And I'd kept my word, and hadn't carved my initials on his face. But I *did* cut him. Because he needed to learn that there were consequences to being a shithead. He now sported a straight line down his right cheek, all the way to his chin. He'd be scarred. Not in a sexy fashion, but in a way that would make him look lopsided forever. He'd hate that.

Good. He'd known Ian was alive that whole time and had never told me. If I did ever see him again, I'd cut more of him up.

I quickened my pace, spotting the exit flanked by guards. The Tradenaline still pumped in my veins and I gave way to it, my feet flying, shadows clinging closely to me.

This was the first real lead I had for Ian. Rachel's notes, and Blake's smartphone. I felt certain that one of those two things held answers. A way forward. A way to save my friend.

Ian.

I'd come back for Rachel. My other friend. But first, I'd finish what we'd started.

I neared the guard station. Gorsel stood watch, of course. Just my luck. And another operative whose name I think was Jane.

I just had to clear them…

Just then, their radio chirped to life and a lockdown alert sounded.

"Like hell," I mumbled, reaching down to retrieve my darts. I whipped one straight at Jane. She dropped like a rock, which made me giggle, because Gorsel was the one who was a rock. Her falling distracted him from hitting the lockdown button for the split second it took me to throw the door open and slip out.

My shadows were momentarily weakened by the bright sunlight that hammered down on the alley.

What the hell was wrong with this alley that it couldn't respect my shadows?

Gorsel simultaneously reached for me and the

lockdown button in a panic. I threw myself down and he just missed me. The door slammed shut.

Ha. Now he was stuck in there. Time to move, though. I doubted it would take them long to reopen the door and come after me. For once grateful for the Tradenaline, I started running down the alley, pulling every shadow tightly around me, intending to get as far from there as possible.

If even half the stories about the fate of rogue Traded were true, it was really best that they never catch me.

16

THE STREETS WOBBLED BEFORE ME, bright and treacherous, filled with people and cars. I rarely went out during the day since shadows were damn hard to find under the treacherous sun. I blinked, cobwebs blocking my vision, my mind reeling like a kaleidoscope as I carefully avoided walking into people.

I loved how much more shiny everyone was in the daylight. A woman sporting a neon pink jacket and orange knee-high boots made me fall even *more* in love with bright colors.

My breath rattled and I landed on my knees. *Keep moving. They're coming.* I managed to stand back up, but the street seemed to be leaning as I walked painstakingly towards the buildings, stealing what few shadows I could to stay hidden. It took what little concentration I had left.

Stupid Tradenaline. I'd taken this dose too close to

the last one. My system wasn't going into overdrive. In fact, it was downright crashing.

*Not here not here not here...*even the simple mantra proved difficult to follow. I didn't know how long I'd been walking when I looked up to where I'd automatically headed.

Clay's guild.

Of course. The one person in the world I could still trust. The one person who could keep me safe.

I slipped in the door and immediately dropped my shadows. The two guards jumped, but quickly recognized me.

"Tira," Sam said, all muscle and blue spikey hair.

"I love your hair," I blurted out. Why was the floor suddenly sideways?

"Easy, girl," The next thing I knew, Sam was holding me.

"I don't really hug," I mumbled, and he nodded.

"I know. Hang on."

"Is that Tira?" I recognized Jolene and smiled.

"Joooleeennnne!" I said, surprised to find myself in a chair. How the hell had that happened?

"Tira, sugar, what happened?" She knelt beside me and placed her hand on my forehead. Her eyes were all serious.

"You smell pretty," I said. I used to hate her scent, which was much too sweet. But she was nice. She called me sugar and sounded like she meant it in a kind way, not in a "I'm making fun of you way."

I liked that.

"I like you," I said, and Jolene smiled, though that

smile didn't quite reach her eyes. She looked worried as she checked my vitals.

It was so nice to be fussed over that I teared up. I really liked this place. I should have just followed Clay. Not that I could have, but it was nice to think that maybe this could have been my home, too.

"Tira," Jolene asked in a clear voice that commanded attention. I focused on her face, framed by perfect blond hair. She'd look smashing in neon pink. "What happened?"

"I took Tradenaline," I said, my words slurring. "Twice in three days."

"Tira," Jolene's perfect features rearranged into a frown, "that's too much for your system, sugar."

"I know, but everyone was trying to kill me," I said, my eyes slowly shutting, though I'd have much preferred continuing to stare at Jolene. "Can I see Clay now?"

"He's finishing up a match," Jolene said. "I'll get him right after, promise."

"Okie dokie."

"Tira," Sam said, his gruff voice to my right. I didn't remember this place being so confusing before. "Is anyone going to come looking for you?"

I blinked and tried to focus on him. "Probably," I sounded sullen even in my own ears. "If I can just rest awhile, I can leave right after."

"Don't worry about that, sugar," Jolene said, as she exchanged a quick glance with Sam. He vanished down the hallway. "No friend of Clay's is going to get turned away."

"That's nice," my words drifted on the edge of my consciousness. I could feel someone lifting me up, though I knew it wasn't Clay.

"I don't hug," I mumbled and then finally drifted away.

I WOKE up in the darkness, senses immediately alert. The Tradenaline was still messing with my head—the whole room tilted as I tried to sit up.

"Tira," Clay's familiar form appeared beside me, gently coaxing me back down. "Lie down. You need to sleep this off real bad."

I let him push me back down on the bed, which smelled of Clay—wildness and strength. Comfort and safety.

He laid down beside me and I shifted closer to him, turning so I could hide against him. Even in near darkness, I found comfort in his shadows. His hand awkwardly wrapped around my waist.

"Who did this to you, Tira?" he said, voice trembling slightly.

"I did," I whispered. Before he could prod further, I settled into him and fell fast asleep to the sound of his beating heart.

I WOKE UP IN DARKNESS, alone.

But I felt a thousand times better. Keeping the lights off, I did some light stretches, testing my body to see if I had any outstanding injuries. I was glad to discover that I had no pain other than the usual "stop running into battles so enthusiastically" legacy wounds. Everything felt a bit muffled, but that was normal while coming down from Tradenaline.

I really hated the stuff. Sucked the life out of you and left you all clammy and gross.

Speaking of which...I switched on a light, smiling at the sight of Clay's room. His battle stats were on the wall, along with a smart board where he'd been thinking up new moves. Clever.

This was a far cry from the clean and sterile rooms of the Guild of Shadows. This room screamed Clay, and I immediately loved it. His desk was covered in notes, his bookshelf with trophies. And, on the main trophy shelf, the central spot of honor, he kept a small framed picture of the two of us.

The only one we had, taken years ago at the Margrave Academy, on one of our Exploration Days (aka road trips to see if guilds were interested in any of us). He looked semi non-grumpy, and I grinned from ear to ear, holding cotton candy. My first ever!

I hadn't realized Clay had kept that picture. We looked so young. So full of hope.

He kept that picture because he still cares for me, like I knew he did. I smiled and noticed a note near the picture, like Clay had known it would draw my eye.

Got match. Come see if you can!

I took a quick shower and headed out of the room, hair still wet, to see if I could find the match. My shadows wrapped instinctively around me. I justified it as not being rude, but cautious. I didn't want to get anyone in trouble, and I knew that the Watch was probably after me.

Not to mention the Guild of Shadows.

Cheering drew me down a corridor, then down several flights of stairs, until I found myself standing at the perimeter of the Wolf Pack's arena. It looked similar to the last time I'd seen it: below me stood a large pit for fighting. Rows of cheering spectators surrounded it, rising up into the rafters. Those were new. Still, even more noise came from the virtual watchers who placed bets on the fighters.

I grinned when I noticed how many more bets had been placed on Clay's win. He had the trust of the crowd. Then I stared down at the arena. They'd put in some ruin-like architecture, to make the terrain more difficult and interesting. Clay, dressed all in black with his hair tied back, pulled out his favorite axe and blocked a blow from a muscular, mostly naked man who wielded a broadsword. His large, red-scaled tail, tipped with a deadly bundle of spikes, screamed "Traded."

He looked big and mean, and much too dangerous for Clay. Yet to me, it was clear that Clay easily had the upper hand. The crowd might not have been able to tell. They cheered wildly with every blow he landed, and gasped nervously when he narrowly avoided a hit. But I could tell he was playing to the crowd, loving every minute of their reactions. He faked left and struck right, landing a blow to his opponent's shin with the hilt of his axe before withdrawing. He could have finished him there and then, but Clay was enjoying it.

I glanced up toward the throne of the Boss, who seemed pleased by the performance, though perhaps a little bored. Her finger traced the rim of her purple cocktail.

It was clear that Clay was ready for the big leagues. But those battles were to the death. And Clay had promised me he wouldn't take that risk. I looked back at him, seeing the laziness of his movements.

He was bored. So was the Boss. And, eventually, the audience would clue in that he wasn't being challenged, and his ratings would drop.

What would happen then? When a fighter was of no more use to his league? Did they just get rid of them? Retire them?

I'd seen their fighters fall, before. Dying in a match wasn't heroic. It was sad, perishing under the watchful stare of a betting board, to be remembered as a money maker or loser.

But Clay seemed to love the battles. The spotlight. The accolades.

I looked back toward the Boss. She had angular features, short-trimmed hair and piercing eyes that always made me feel like I was too noticeable in her presence. Even my shadows didn't feel like enough cover. Except I knew that she couldn't see me, no matter how much she made my skin crawl.

So far, aside from Glitter, only Lorna, an older Guild operative, had been able to see through my shadows. And she was gone, taken by the same people who had taken Ian.

And she'd been just as abandoned as Ian.

Footsteps echoed down the corridor. I automatically hid Rachel's laptop and stood up. Relief flooded me as Clay stepped in, shirtless and sweaty, no scar or wound to speak of. His eyes lit up at the sight of me and he broke into a giant grin, crossing the room and gathering me in a hug.

It was kind of gross, but also kind of nice. He remembered that we didn't really hug and he let me go. But his hands lingered on my shoulders and he stayed close, dark eyes seeking mine out.

"What kind of trouble are you in, Tira?" His voice was so serious, so laced with concern, that I felt bad for bringing my troubles to his doorstep.

"I'm sorry. I shouldn't have come here, Clay. That was stupid."

"Hey," he stopped me, squeezing my shoulders, "I'm glad you came here. You were pretty doped up."

"Thanks," I mumbled. "But trouble might follow. I

mean, it probably will. They'll know I came here. I don't have any other friend except you."

Clay ignored the implication behind my words. "Who's they? Who's coming after you, Tira?" A slight growl slipped into his words, his fangs visible under his curled lip.

"I…I'm not sure. It's kind of a long story."

"Tell me," Clay insisted, coaxing me to sit down on the bed and shifting so he could look at me. I sighed, and told him about how I'd messed up Blake. But I didn't mention the Watch, not wanting to implicate Clay any more than I already had. Clay was pretty pleased I'd bested Blake, and didn't think to ask too many questions. I knew he wouldn't. Clay had never asked enough questions, really.

Then I mentioned that the Guild might also be coming after me.

"Do you think they'd really come after you?" Clay asked, and I could hear the "I told you so" lingering on his lips. I mean, he wasn't wrong. But it didn't mean I wanted to hear it.

"I'm not sure, honestly," I said. "I mean, I broke rules. If Ian was there, he could protect me, but…" I stopped. I hadn't told Clay Ian was gone.

"Ian's not there?" I was pretty sure this was the first time I heard Clay say Ian's actual name.

"He got taken," I had to look away and focused on the floor. This was the moment I'd been dreading. If Clay was glad that Ian was gone—if his eyes flashed with victory because of it—I wouldn't be able to take it.

"Who took him?" he asked, his voice even more soft.

I chanced a look his way, and only saw concern in his eyes.

"Same people who took Lorna."

"Oh," he absorbed the information, then hesitated before asking the next question. "When did they take him?"

I started to doubt the logic behind keeping this all from Clay. There was obvious hurt in his eyes. I stood up.

"I'm sorry, Clay. I really should go." He followed me up and nodded before starting to pack some gear.

"Be ready in five," he said, grabbing snacks from his cupboard. And money! Clay was way more equipped than I was.

"Wait, what?" I managed to spit out.

"You're going after Ian. You've got no guild. But you've got me," he shrugged. "So, I'm coming."

"You don't have to come," I stumbled. "You probably shouldn't come with me, in fact. I'm the only one who should have to deal with the consequences of my stupidity."

"You'll need my help to find Ian," he said matter-of-factly. "Besides, I don't have a fight for another few days. Might as well take a mini vacay."

The jaunty way he said vacay drew a slight laugh from me, which seemed to please him.

"I didn't think you liked Ian," I whispered as he finished gathering his things.

"I don't," he said, "but you're my friend. And whatever trouble you're about to get yourself into, I'm in."

"How do you know I'll even go after him? It's been weeks, Clay."

He threw on a fresh shirt and shrugged into a coat. "Because you don't give up on your friends, Tira," he focused on me, dark eyes deadly serious, "and neither do I. "Another grin, slightly forced, found his lips. "And, if we see Blake, we can take him down together."

I bit my lip, vowing to tell him about the Watch as soon as we were somewhere safe. Clay was my friend, and I should just tell him. But knowing seemed so dangerous. I hesitated, not sure how much he needed to know. How much he *should* know.

"Now, come on," he said, throwing the door open. "This will be just like old times."

"Just like old times," I repeated as I followed him out of the room. Sure, just like old times.

Except, this time, I was the one hoarding all the secrets.

20

CLAY LOOKED annoyed as I left him to keep an eye out. I didn't know how well-guarded the embassy would be after two attacks, but I figured it would be pretty impenetrable. Unless you were basically invisible. Evening dropped over the city and the shadows came easily to me. I'd only been gone from the Guild for seven hours, though it felt longer.

The Tradenaline had knocked me out like usual. But for a little bit less time. I hated thinking I was getting used to it, but at the same time, it had saved my ass with Blake.

Or had it? I doubted Blake would have killed me. But he wouldn't have told me what he'd known about Ian if I hadn't gained the edge on him. Grabbing a windowsill, I disabled the alarm with a handy hack disk from the Guild, and opened the lock with a careful picking. The window slid outward silently. I waited a few moments, and no alarm sounded, nor did anyone scream. Good signs, both.

I'd studied the grounds of the embassy thoroughly for escape routes. This window was off the library, and provided great shadows no matter where the sun was in the sky. If the Guild of Shadows had taught me one thing, it was that each operative had to play to their own strengths. And everyone had been selected to bring something different to the table.

An unexpected sorrow blossomed in my chest at the thought of the Guild of Shadows. I'd never really felt like I'd belonged, so why should I feel bad about losing it? But I did, because I'd been starting to build a home. Until Ian had been taken, anyway.

I'd give up a thousand guilds to get my friend back.

I slipped quietly past two guards, then skirted the wall toward Aia's study. Security barriers blocked its crumbling and charred remains.

Rachel had done a number on it. The papers on Aia's desk were as charred as the walls. But Aia had carried her tablet out with her, so I had to hope she had backup documents on there. I glanced around, a light emanating from a room on the other side of the sitting area.

Aia had liked it here because she wanted to be as far away from her father and the dignitaries as possible. I wasn't sure why—it wasn't my job to know. I just needed to know how she might react to stressors so I could plan for them.

Another lesson from the Guild of Shadows.

The door was partly opened, providing easy access. It was a study, similar but bigger than Aia's blown up one, with a conversation area composed of three couches and a larger desk at the end. Only a few candles had been lit, as though to cast the illusion that the room was smaller. Aia sat on one of the couches, reading files from her tablet.

Shit.

I'd been hoping I could just grab the tablet, preferably discarded and unwatched. That had been a lot to hope for, but I loved hoping.

Listing my options didn't prove very helpful. I could knock her out, but I didn't want to waste another sleeping dart when I was already running low. It's not like the Guild would be handing me extras. A quick hit to the back of the neck would also incapacitate her, but humans were pretty squishy and I didn't want to risk it.

Shit shit shit.

Besides, she'd seemed pretty nice.

Looks can be deceptive.

But I was a demon, and I could be deceptive, too. After all, I looked like a demon, but I was deceptively fun.

I couldn't waffle forever, so I quietly closed the door to give us some privacy. I did a once around and debated if I could just grab the tablet from her hands. I mean, I probably could. She wouldn't see me coming. But she'd know who it was, and the Guild of Shadows —or worse, the Watch—would have another lead on me. The more breadcrumbs I left behind, the easier I'd be to find.

There was one other, simple way. I'd have to trust her.

This is going to suck.

I sat on the couch in front of her and dropped my shadows. She looked startled, but didn't scream. Thankfully.

"Hi," I said, feeling way too vulnerable. There might as well have been a spotlight on me, even though only a few atmospheric candles lit the room.

"You're alright," she looked genuinely relieved.

"I am." It hadn't occurred to me that she would have been worried about me.

"Thanks for saving my life," she placed the tablet on her lap and focused on me. Damn it. Why couldn't she have set it down on the couch?

I shrugged. "I was just doing my job."

Wanting to avoid further small talk and fold back into my shadows, I decided to just get to the point. It couldn't be worse than chit-chatting while sitting here, completely visible and vulnerable.

"Can I borrow your tablet?" My use of the term borrow was fast and loose, but I might be able to return it someday. Her eyebrow shot up and she clutched the tablet to her chest. That wasn't promising.

"I promise I won't hurt you," I said, holding up my hands. "I could have just taken it, but I chose to chat with you instead. And I hate dropping my shadows."

Her suspicion partly melted into amusement, and possibly sympathy. Hard to tell, because few people had ever looked at me that way.

"Why do you want it?" she asked. Her voice was soft, as though intent on not alarming the guards. Or possibly to appease me—she must have known how easy it would have been for me to eviscerate her.

"To save my friend," I replied, equally softly.

"Your friend is in trouble?" she leaned forward in interest. I couldn't figure her out, but I didn't think she was a bad or even a mean person.

"He is," I said. I debated keeping secrets from her, but couldn't figure out how to convince her otherwise. Besides, I figured a diplomat's daughter had to be pretty good at picking up bullshit. "He was taken by some bad guys, who also took some of the people I saw on your papers earlier. I figured there might be a backup of those documents on your tablet."

Her eyes widened even more, then narrowed as she studied me.

"Who sent you?" she asked softly, though I detected no fear in her voice. Maybe I'd underestimated her squishiness.

"Um, no one," I said. "I made pretty much everyone mad, including the Guild of Shadows. I think the only place people would send me now would be like, Traded jail, whatever that is."

"There's no jail, Tira," Aia said softly. "They will just kill you if you break out of your guild. You know that, right?"

I shrugged. "Figured as much. I was just trying to make it easier for you, I guess."

"Doesn't it bother you? How dispensable they decided you are?"

"I need those files, please. Ian is one of my only friends, and he's worth the risk."

She hesitated, still clutching the tablet to her chest. "Who is this Ian?"

He wasn't in her files. My stomach dropped a bit. Maybe I was barking up the wrong tree? Maybe her files didn't matter at all. I was getting more and more uncomfortable—I hated these chairs that squished my tail against my back.

Nobody ever thought of demons when building chairs.

"He's the second-in-command of the Guild of Shadows. Or was, I suppose. But he's missing. Has been for almost four weeks."

Aia's words were spoken so gently they felt like chocolate. I'd only had it once, but that's what her voice sounded like, right now. "Tira, you know your friend might already be dead, right?"

I nodded. "I know, but I don't think so. Someone from the Watch told me he was still alive."

"You know someone from the Watch?" she leaned forward this time, so excited the tablet seemed forgotten in her hands.

"I do, though we're not friends. He's a douchebag," I said, still loving the sound of that word.

"Could you introduce us?" She asked, with a tad more despair than I would have anticipated.

"Um, I beat him up and embarrassed him, so he probably wants to kill me. But, if he doesn't kill me on sight, I'll totally ask." That didn't sound very plausible.

She shook her head. "No, never mind, don't risk it. But, if you learn anything else from the Watch, would you be willing to tell me?"

"I guess? Will you lend me the tablet?"

She took a deep breath and looked down at it. "I

have a backup, so I don't want you to think these are the only copies."

"Okay." Permission to break tablet: check.

"But if people find out I have these documents, there will be hell to pay. And I'll be the one paying it." Her eyes met mine, dark and determined, but vulnerable, too. Like she'd just dropped some of her own shadows.

I leaned forward, wanting to make her feel better. I resisted the urge to draw my shadows around us both, to protect us from enemies closing in.

"I don't want to get you in trouble," I said, meaning every word. "I really just want to get my friend back."

"I know," she said with a tired smile. It vanished as quickly as it had appeared. "But there are many things happening, Tira, and not everything is at it seems. You must be careful."

"Worry about yourself," I said. "You're the one the assassins are gunning for." For a split second, I almost asked her if she wanted to come with me, but realized I couldn't keep her safe. I wasn't really sure I could keep *me* safe.

"I will, Tira Misu, if you will do the same." When she said my name, it didn't make me cringe. She stood and slipped beside me on the couch. Not close enough to touch me, but much closer. Her face looked older, wiser, and kinder.

I wanted to lose myself in her warmth. But I sat stiffly, afraid to touch her, too.

"Here," Aia said softly, handing me the tablet. "All I ask is that you come tell me that you're safe once you return," she waited for me to nod. "The password is...Amelia."

"That's a beautiful name," I said softly.

"It is," she whispered. She swallowed hard, then stood again. I followed suit, the whole room stifling with unspent emotions, leaving me eager to get out of here and head back into the cover of the cool night and my shadows.

"Thank you," I whispered as I called my shadows and slipped out her window, hoping against hope that we'd both live long enough to see each other again.

———

21

CLAY PACED AROUND ME, throwing glances outside from time to time as I examined the various pieces of the puzzle. In the Guild of Shadows, they encouraged you to analyze the facts, scout, weigh perceived threats, report back. To be smart and blend in. To go undetected.

The Wolf Pack League taught its fighters to hit first and ask questions later. A perfect fit for Clay.

We'd hunkered down in an old guild, destroyed by Glitter's gang. Cordoned off and forgotten, like the Traded who'd died here didn't even matter. Blood stains hadn't even been washed off the walls. But at least some rooms had been untouched.

Like the one we now occupied. It contained a quaint bed and desk in an easily defensible part of the abandoned building. There was a great view of the city from the window.

The sun would rise in a few hours. We'd either make our move tonight, or sleep during the day and head out the following night. Delaying for a day seemed dangerous, with so many people after us. So many highly skilled, super angry people.

"You sure he's still alive?" Clay asked, and I nodded.

"For now. Blake said they were being used for some sort of experiment. Older Traded. The ones who came here before the rest of us."

"Ian came here before us?"

I nodded absentmindedly. "A few years before, yeah."

"Huh. Older guy, eh?" I ignored what he was trying to infer.

"Aia's files are just about older Traded."

"So, she didn't know they were kidnapped?" Clay shot a glance my way before focusing back on the night. He sighed and closed the window coverings again. I'd argued he would give us away by revealing our light, but he'd mumbled something about keeping watch.

"Doesn't seem to know. But she was aware of the Watch. She seemed to be doing research into where these Traded first appeared."

I grabbed Blake's half-hacked phone. I'd grabbed the smart phone, which served as his gaublet (smashed, thanks to me), pulling out the SIM card so it would be untraceable. But he'd passed out before I'd gotten the code out of him. I had some quick hack software, but nothing in depth. Just stuff for field operatives to be able to break into systems. His was pretty damn well protected, but his map software was more vulnerable.

And, thankfully, Blake seemed to have relied heavily on it.

His words rang in my mind, annoyingly clear. *Last I saw him, he looked ready to cross death's door.* Still, Ian had been alive. *Was* alive.

Blake really sucked, and his only saving grace was his reliance on his GPS. Not that it would save him from me cutting him more. The next clue would be somewhere in those addresses, and the gathered notes.

It had to be—it was all we had.

Rachel's notes included a few locations, too. Places with weird sightings or occurrences, like people suddenly abandoning homes, or entire neighborhoods selling their places at once, handing their lives to investors without any clear reason why. She'd built on my initial research, adding layers of thinking. Rachel was a pretty smart cookie.

She'd followed the investor trail but that had quickly grown cold, with too many shell companies doing the purchases. But she'd looked at the various places across the city, and had always found a Traded or two just hanging around. That was odd. They looked human, but Rachel was well trained. And Traded tended to stand out in one way or another, no matter how hard they tried to blend in.

There were places where Traded were "free," (not part of a guild but under strict watch), and these were nowhere near there. That meant someone had placed them there. Or some*thing*, like a guild.

Between Blake's map, Rachel's notes, and Aia's documents, I ended up with a bunch of addresses.

Could it be that easy?

Clay cracked his knuckles and dropped to the ground to do pushups.

I started to correlate the three sources, looking for locations that were the same across all three lists. It took a few minutes, since there were so many, but nothing came up. I double-checked, but again, no luck. I stood and stretched.

"Anything?" Clay asked, pushing himself back up, jumping up and down where he stood like he was warming up for fight. Which, I suppose, he was.

"Not yet," I said, "but I think I'm getting close."

"Great!" he said, and fell back down for more pushups.

I sat back at the desk and looked for places that showed up on two lists, finding six different spots. Five of those were shared by Aia's and Blake's lists. Rachel shared one spot with Aia, and one spot with both of them.

Blake had said "when last I'd seen Ian." Which could have been a while ago, and he couldn't recall where exactly, that he'd hardly cared enough to pay attention.

I should have cut him more.

The address they all shared was marked as having had an earlier portal, fifty years ago. A whole thirty years before the massive trade that had brought my generation of Traded to this planet.

Were the original Traded even called Traded? According to Ian, they weren't swapped for humans. They'd just appeared, and not as babies like us, either. They were slightly older, some full-grown.

Ian hadn't remembered much from his home world, so he must have been pretty young when he'd arrived. But he did remember some things, which was more than the rest of us could say.

When he'd arrived, he'd been found by Sonsil. He hadn't been reported or recorded. Maybe that was why he wasn't on Aia's list. And everyone on her list was older than Ian. He must have been one of the last ones to appear before the giant swap.

I rubbed my temples, feeling just at the edge of a breakthrough. Or at least a decision…

I looked at Rachel's information. The location she shared with Aia was a small, abandoned mall, in the middle of an older neighborhood. The property had been sold ten years ago, and never reopened. By all accounts, it had been left derelict. But Rachel had jotted notes, with dates of police calls and reported strange occurrences.

Things that might lead people to believe that a Traded lurked in the area.

I looked at the name of the buyer, underlined by Rachel: Infinity Corporation. My blood ran cold. Infinity, like the symbol representing the Guild of Shadows.

Not everything is as it seems.

"Got something?" Clay asked. I jumped. He loomed over my shoulder, looking at my notes, having sensed that I was drawing near a conclusion.

"I think so," I said. "But I'm not sure." I didn't feel like having him tell me again that the Guild of Shadows sucked. Besides, that wasn't the best lead.

The best lead was the one shared by all three. A car dealership in the industrial district. Aia hadn't provided any reason for marking the site. Neither had Blake. But Rachel had jotted down reports of strange activities, the low sales numbers, and frequent closures.

"Okay," I took a deep breath. "I think I've got it."

"Awesome!" He exclaimed.

"We should be careful," I said. "Glitter might be there. He's way more powerful than he has any right to be." I remembered him controlling me with his powers, pushing my dread deep down.

"So you say," he shrugged. "But he won't get me as easily as Ian. Sorry," he quickly added.

"It's not that," I said, not bothering to tell Clay how injured Ian had been when he'd been taken. "It's the magic. He can control minds. Make you do things. Gotta be careful not to run into him, or if we do, to take him out damn fast. And we don't know how many allies he'll have."

Clay nodded, jumping in place like he was about to head into a boxing ring.

"Got it. Punch first, ask questions later."

I sighed and shook my head, grabbing what few weapons I had. My sword. A few daggers. Three remaining darts. Clay handed me a weird looking gun. "Like a taser on overdrive," he grinned. "You'll love it. Just don't zap yourself."

I grinned back as he threw on more weapons than I could count. Clay wasn't exactly the stealthy type. That was more my style.

"Clay," I placed my hand on his arm as he started

making his way toward the door. He stopped and stared at me. "Just…just promise me you'll be careful."

He grinned. "Always am!"

And he crossed to the door. I sighed. I was glad he was here and I wasn't going in there alone. I just hoped that he'd remember the main goal of the mission, which was to save the guy he couldn't stand. Hopefully Clay wouldn't just become a one-man demolition crew.

Ah well. The punching would come in pretty handy, too.

22

Disable alarm: check.

Turn off power: check.

Pick lock: check.

This place wasn't so bad, but it all felt too easy. Like we were walking into a trap. Or, worse, no one cared if we stumbled into their weird lab, because everyone was already dead. Just like at the convenience store.

Lines of shiny cars led to empty offices.

"You sure it's here?" Clay asked, clutching his axe, already looking impatient.

"I'm not sure, no. I mean, it's a best guess. But let's scout it out, see what we find." I headed to the back of the lunchroom and into some storerooms, careful to stay quiet though the place looked deserted.

Clay had strayed across the room, scanning the room for any signs of life.

"Stay close so I can keep my shadows around you," I said, annoyed. Clay shrugged, but came closer.

"You think that's necessary?"

"We don't know if they have cameras," I huffed. That was a lie. I *did* know they had cameras, and I'd made sure they were off. I really missed gaublet. If I knew how to unhook him from the Guild network, I'd use him, but I couldn't risk the Guild, or the Watch, following our trail. Thankfully, their cameras had been easy to turn off by means of a main switch under the front desk.

The ease with which I'd disabled them only made me all the more suspicious. I glanced at the safety evacuation plan on the wall. Sometimes, these gave away hidden exits and entrances. But this one was dead simple, since this place was all windows and doors.

"In the convenience store," I whispered, squinting at the map, "there was a basement, where they did their experiments. Behind a big fancy metal door."

"Like this one?" Clay practically hollered from the other room. He'd stepped out of my shadows without my noticing.

"Damn it, Clay," I mumbled as I joined him, wrapping my shadows around him again. He gave me an apologetic shrug, which would have been more effective if he didn't have his "getting it done, you can thank me later" look on his face.

I ignored him and turned to analyze the door. Rachel had hacked the last door to let me in. This one seemed to have the same locking mechanism. That was great—it meant we were on the right track. But it also sucked, because I didn't have Rachel, or even gaublet, to help out.

"Want me to help?" Clay asked beside me, moving from side to side, jittery for action.

Another long sigh escaped me. "Can you do it quietly?"

"I can make it quick," he answered. It was the best we had, so I moved aside, wincing as he struck the control panel hard, smashing it.

The door clicked open.

Another "getting it done" grin.

"Let me go first," I said. He didn't budge. "Last one was the same set-up, and there were no traps. I can make sure I'm not seen. I'll duck if anything bad comes at us, and you can hit it. How's that?"

He didn't seem overly convinced, but finally stepped aside.

I squeezed his arm as I passed him, reassuring him that we had this. His grin told me he got the message, his hand tightening around his axe.

"It's not that I don't trust you," he said. "It's just that, you know, if he's here, I don't want you to see him. Not like that. That's all."

My heart skipped a beat. My breath faltered. I nodded.

I'd thought of that, too. But I wanted to stick with Sonsil's philosophy and believe (stubbornly and unrelentingly) that Ian still lived. Not trusting my voice, I squeezed his arm again and slipped down the stairs. Clay stayed close behind me.

This basement was much bigger. A hallway led to a bigger, dimly lit room up ahead. Several doors flanked the corridor. Clay and I shared a quick glance and began clearing them, one by one. This might be our only exit, so we had to make sure it would remain clear.

Clay went in, and I kept watch outside, ready to help or shout a warning if anyone arrived. The little I saw within those rooms turned my stomach. More beakers and science-y stuff. Boat loads of medicines, too. I had no clue what any of it was for, but it was clear that it wasn't for good. Metal pans. Metal beds. All waiting for their next victim.

Clay looked more and more grim. I'm sure my expression matched his. Even my tail didn't bother twitching with worry. The whole world just felt too heavy right now.

With all six rooms cleared, only the large room ahead of us was left.

Stay close, I mouthed to him, gathering my shadows more tightly as we stepped into the cavernous room. Several stark lights dangled from the ceiling, challenging my shadows. Heavy machines and conveyor belts obscured my view of the back of the room.

Clay raised an eyebrow as we headed in, following the line of conveyor belts. The black rollers seemed slick with something. It was too dark to make out what, but the stench of death was undeniable.

What the hell were they doing here?

I found myself moving more quickly. We needed to clear this place, fast…Clay grabbed my arm and stopped me. He pointed down, where the conveyor belt dipped into a chute.

The stench wafting up made my eyes water.

"Stay here," he whispered, and carefully made his way down, until he was out of sight.

A minute passed. And another. I stood frozen in place. I waited for Clay to return. To tell me he'd found Ian, or what remained of him.

But it wasn't Clay's voice that made me move.

It was Blake's.

23

"Demon girl," Blake smiled at me, but it held no warmth.

"Hey, pretty boy," I smiled at him, looking pointedly at the red, angry cut running down his face. I did great work under pressure.

His eyes darkened further. "You come alone? No backup? Tsk tsk. That's how Traded get dead, you know."

Good. They hadn't spotted Clay. I didn't want him and his league to get in trouble because of me.

I maintained my casual stance, shrugging at Blake. "I didn't think I needed back up against the likes of you."

I made sure to stay far enough away from him that I could avoid his powers, or so I hoped. He took a step forward, the conveyor belt standing between us. I took out my cool taser gun. "Don't get closer."

"Afraid I'll take you down?"

"Honestly not willing to take the risk."

I really hoped Clay wouldn't choose now to reappear. I forced myself to keep staring at Blake instead of glancing back worriedly. Sure, Clay's league fought to the death. But in arenas.

That suddenly seemed tame compared to what the Watch would do.

"Tell you what," I said, "why don't we just part ways. No hard feelings?"

"You think it would be that easy?" his voice rumbled with a threat, unlike anything I'd ever heard before. "Oh, Tira, I'm going to enjoy hurting you."

Behind me, I heard a movement. I whipped around, where stood one of his cronies, hand aimed toward me like a gun. Energy gathered around his fingers and I jumped sideways, too late to avoid the blast that sent me flying toward Blake. I grabbed the edge of the conveyor belt and flipped up, my wrist flicking a dart toward him. But he was ready, stopping it with his powers.

My dart wasn't the only thing he stopped. He caught me just as my feet touched the ground, before I could regain my footing and strike.

He didn't just hold me there. He crushed my lungs until I couldn't draw breath.

"It would be easy to kill you," he hissed as he walked up beside me. "No one would care. Your Guild leader is in jail for letting a rogue agent escape." I would have gasped if I could have breathed. *Sonsil.* I'd never considered that he'd pay a price. "The Guild of

Shadows is over. Done. Its operatives will be redirected to other guilds. Probably circus guilds."

He smirked at me, knowing he'd hit home. Fury and grief mixed with lack of oxygen as I grit my teeth, desperately calling on my shadows. They barely shifted. I was too weakened by the lack of air. A dark tunnel slowly collapsed around my vision. I forced myself to calm down, to win a bit more time before passing out.

I didn't think passing out would help my situation.

"You, however," he leaned in, hot breath on my face, "will get the honor of being dealt with by me."

He struck, hard, and I collapsed. I managed to draw a deep breath as I pivoted to strike, but he held up his hand, stopping my motion.

"Tsk, tsk, Tira. You really should learn to relax a bit more."

"Beating on you would relax me," I managed to say through gritted teeth.

"Mmm, it's nice to see your spirit isn't broken," he said, then smiled what I supposed he thought was a charming smile. "Just like your friend! What was her name? Rachel? Anyway, she didn't talk," his head tilted, the shadows highlighting the cruelty in his features. "She's dead."

I hissed at him, narrowing my eyes, hot tears gathering at my eyes. "I don't believe you," I managed to say, voice low and steady. And full of hatred.

"She tried to fight," he said, cocking his head. A tear escaped my eye (damn it), and he reached out with his hand and gathered it on his finger. *Creep.* "She almost blew up on us, you know," a smirk as he pulled out a dark stained knife. "Stabbed her through the heart before she could."

Something deep within me snapped. Rage flooded me. I wanted him to die, so bad. He'd hurt me. I'd hurt him. But he'd had no right to kill Rachel. To kill my *friend!*

He must have sensed the shift in me, and a flicker of worry suddenly lit his eyes. I reached deep for my shadows, calling them to me in spite of his hold on me. They came, and I slammed them into him.

He didn't see them coming, flying back against a wall, he bounced hard and crumpled to the ground. His hold on me vanished.

"Down!" Clay's voice rang out, and I ducked as a blast warmed my shoulder.

A wet noise, and the man with blaster hands was down, Clay's axe having severed his jugular.

"What the hell was that?" he demanded. I grabbed his hand and started pulling him away.

"Tira!" He said, pulling his hand out of mine.

"Clay, please," I pleaded, voice harsh, lungs hurting, despair filling every word. "There might be more on the way. We need to go."

He examined me for a moment longer and simply nodded. I wrapped my shadows around him and we started making our way out, our pace increasing with every step.

I don't think I breathed until we were completely

out of the district. Even then, I kept looking over my shoulder, remembering Blake's words.

Sonsil was gone. The Guild disbanded. Its operatives sent to other guilds. Rachel was dead.

What had I done?

WE WALKED IN SILENCE. I kept us wrapped in shadows, as I kept my heart wrapped in grief. Finally, we stopped near a quieter shopping district, mostly closed now except for a few restaurants. We slipped into an alley between two buildings, which led to a little courtyard between closed shops.

As soon as I felt a modicum of safety, I leaned against the wall and lowered myself to the ground, hugging my knees to my chest. My shadows vanished, fatigue draping around my mind.

Clay crouched in front of me, placing a hand on my knee. "I didn't see him," he said softly. "Or anything that might have been him."

I gazed deep into his eyes, making sure no lie lurked there, and then nodded, biting my lower lip. My breath came in a spasm as I unsuccessfully tried to push away the emotions threatening to overwhelm me.

Tears started pouring out of me, like I'd grown a leak.

"I swear I'm not lying," Clay said, eyes wide. "I swear!"

A laugh escaped me, interspersed with the sobs. I forced myself to take a deep breath.

"I believe you," I said. "It's just...the Guild of Shadows is gone, Clay. Sonsil is in jail. Everyone is scattered, or dead. I don't...I don't know what to do."

To his credit, Clay didn't betray the joy he undoubtedly felt at my guild being broken. But his hand tightened on my knee, like he struggled against his own emotions.

"First, I'm going to get us some food," he said. "Then, we're going to figure everything out, okay?"

He said it so calmly, with such self-assurance, that I felt immediately better. I grabbed his hand as he stood up.

"Be careful. Please." *You're all I have left.*

"I will. Promise." And he stepped out of the alley. I wrapped my shadows back around me in case someone happened to stumble in here, the sounds of life filtering in from the few restaurants down the street.

The neighborhood was seedy enough, and Clay human-looking enough, that he could come and go without question. Not me. Not the demon girl, as Blake so gently put it.

I stood up and stretched, numbness creeping into my tired body. I'd done too much, too quickly. And yet, I'd accomplished so little. Hell, I'd focused so much on Ian's needs (which, to be fair, were pretty damn pressing), that I'd firebombed everything else.

The Guild of Shadows. It hadn't been perfect, but it

had been the only home I'd had. What would happen now? Blake wanted me dead. I couldn't keep dragging Clay into this. His league would get involved, and then what? I'd get them all killed?

I reached the edge of the little courtyard, where a scraggly bush stood sentry. Gently, I reached out and touched its leaves, its branches prickling my skin. I wouldn't abandon Ian.

But that didn't mean I would sacrifice Clay, either.

"Hey," Clay said. He couldn't see me, but he could guess where I was. For a split second, I considered keeping my shadows up. Slipping away into the darkness, to let Clay find his own way home. He wouldn't give up on me easily, I knew. But that didn't mean he'd ever find me.

"I know what you're thinking," he said softly. "Let's talk, first. Don't leave me alone to drink this terrible sugary concoction you call coffee."

He knew how to read me, even when he couldn't see me. I dropped my shadows and joined him. We both sat down and I took the offered coffee and croissant, ignoring the glances he cast my way. It was clear he was holding back a question he couldn't quite voice.

The terrible concoction was more cream and sugar than coffee, which was the only way the stuff was tolerable. The croissant went down easily, and I was soon stuffing some kind of egg muffin thing in my mouth. It tasted like sheer heaven, and I began to feel better.

Sensing the shift in me, Clay finally spoke up.

"Tell me about Blake. Why the hell did we run away from him?"

"He's with the Watch," I said softly, afraid of saying the word too loudly.

"The what?"

"The Watch. I don't really know, Clay, except they're kind of in charge of the guilds. Any rogue Traded are dealt with by the Watch."

"Okay," Clay said, taking a bite of a donut and thinking things through before moving ahead. "So why was Blake after you then? What's his problem?" A smile lingered at the corner of his lips "I mean, aside from being a douchebag."

"I got in trouble because I was seen twice by humans," I winced as I described the whole painful embassy mission to him in detail. "So, after, Blake came by to…to punish me. He has the control tattoo codes, Clay. At least mine."

Clay's hand wrapped around mine, like trying to force me to stay focused on him.

"Why couldn't you be seen by humans, Tira?" Clay asked, dark eyes piercing me. Really? Out of everything I'd just said, that was the thing he chose to focus on?

"Because I'm Traded?" I raised an eyebrow.

"So am I," he said, "and my matches are streamed."

"Sure," I shrugged, "but you're not in their living room."

"No," he said, as though still working through it, "but some Traded are, right? Some of the entertainment guilds. And circus guilds. Some are guards at important buildings and stuff. Tira, the

Traded are everywhere. I mean, like, there are a *lot* of us."

"Okay," I said, now also working through it. "Maybe it was the embassy that mattered?"

"But you said the ambassador's daughter wasn't scared of seeing you there? And, they work on Traded stuff. So, then, *why* couldn't you be seen?"

"I don't know!" I said, frustrated, wishing we'd just go back to joking about Blake being a douchebag.

"Hear me out," he said, "I know this is annoying, but, think: have you ever gone out to get a donut?"

"What? Of course not!" The thought of strolling into the donut shop and ordering something was so ludicrous it annoyed me even more.

"I just did. And it's not the first time."

"You can pass for human, Clay, and I can't. You know that."

"I know," he said, lowering his voice. "And I don't want to hurt you. But not everyone in there looks human, you know what I mean?"

"I don't."

"Go look."

I almost told him I wouldn't, but he was so intent that I turned to head to the mouth of the alley. I could tell he wanted to follow me, but he stayed seated. I wrapped my shadows around me and peaked around the corner.

The coffee shop wasn't far. I could see how busy it was inside through the tall windows.

And it wasn't just humans inside. A three-armed, green-skinned guy sat with two other bikers (or whatever they were), sharing a laugh. Something that looked more like a mop than a Traded was having a drink with a human-looking woman. And behind the counter was someone rather too pink in skin tone to be human.

Nobody paid them much mind, either. I felt like a voyeur, though—like they were on display in the brightly lit coffee shop.

I returned to the courtyard and sat down beside Clay, dropping my shadows as my arms hugged my torso. To his credit, he didn't say "I told you so." He'd had a lot of opportunities to say it lately, but hadn't, which I really appreciated.

"Look, all I'm saying is, your guild is the one staying so secretive. The world knows the Traded are here. Most have some kind of life. Some freedoms."

"Your league kills a lot of Traded," I said without any fire. I think I was fresh out.

"Sure," he shrugged, "but lots of humans kill themselves in stupid sports, too. It's just way clearer for us what our purpose is, which isn't so bad. And we get a lot in return. I mean, glory. Money. Lots of freedoms. Just don't step out of line, of course. Because then your life is forfeit."

"Maintain the balance," I muttered.

"Exactly," Clay said, looking pleased that I'd seemingly understood. Except he didn't understand quite *what* I'd understood. The Guild of Shadows was here to maintain the balance. Maybe that was why we were kept hidden. So we wouldn't be known and stopped, sure. So we wouldn't reveal secrets, of course.

And so we'd always be ready to deploy as needed, like some special forces.

Except there was another reason, too. So we wouldn't develop too many attachments to the outside world. Ian had always said that was my greatest weakness. Because the Guild would try to control me through Clay. Just like he thought that Sonsil was trying to leverage me against him. But he wasn't.

No, Clay was a problem because he was *outside* the guild. Because if our allegiances flowed too far from the home base, they might be tested when ordered to take a rogue faction down. Or a rogue Traded.

What if we were kept in the shadows to remain the ultimate weapon?

And what happened now that that weapon had been dismantled by the Watch?

25

WITH A WORTHWHILE AMOUNT of night left to take advantage of, Clay and I headed to the next logical location: the one place on both Aia's and Rachel's lists. If Blake wasn't aware of it, that was even better. I wasn't eager to encounter him again, though Clay seemed to be, cracking his knuckles ominously every time his name came up.

The abandoned strip mall loomed ahead, tall fences erected to keep out loiterers and vandals. Shadows tightly drawn around us, we headed south of the mall. Behind the creepy old mall stood a quaint suburban neighborhood where families slumbered.

Clay is my family. And Ian. The Guild of Shadows could have been, I guessed. Crushing grief threatened to overwhelm me again, so I took a deep breath and gave Clay a playful punch on the shoulder. His surprised look morphed into a grin when he saw mine.

This will work out. We would find Ian. And we'd escape the Watch. Okay, that was too much positive thinking, which could prove dangerous. Don't imagine you've won the battle until the last foe has fallen. Or so the Guild of Shadows had taught me.

Pushing the Guild out of my mind (or trying really hard to), we skirted the perimeter until I found a snare in the fence. A ragged hole, probably cut by some vandals.

Time to head in.

We slipped through the hole in the fence. Clay brimmed with energy beside me, ready to cut something in two. Or, more specifically, cut *someone* in two. Hopefully before they got off a shot.

A door stood open waiting for us. There were no windows to bar our entry, either. They'd long since been shattered. Moonlight lit the way in. It all felt entirely too easy, like we were being funneled in. With handy noisemakers in the form of window shards littering the floor.

Before I could alert Clay, he ducked in, glass crunching loudly under his boots. His face twisted in embarrassment and worry, but he kept moving fast. I moved a bit more carefully, but stayed close enough to extend my shadows around him.

If he was going to make so much noise, the last thing we needed was for him to be visible, too!

Thankfully, the inside seemed deserted. Empty storefronts flanked us, like sentinels, leading the way to a corridor that crossed in front of us, travelling the length of the mall.

The mall itself must have been cute in its day. Wrought iron decorated the store fronts, and the intricately designed glass roof would have allowed shoppers to enjoy the sun on nice days.

Clay looked back at me as though asking "where to?"

I pointed left. As good as any direction, really.

I doubted a mall map would say "portal here!" Although that would be pretty handy.

We crossed two more empty sentinel storefronts and turned left. To our right, beyond the broken gate that used to bar entry to a now-deserted store, green eyes lit up.

Glitter! Glitter, who could see through my shadows with those glowing eyes. I crouched and threw a dagger in his direction, while Clay raised his gun and fired into the darkness, the sound resonating throughout the mall. Had the man never heard of a silencer?

The glowing eyes vanished, and I hoped we'd downed him.

Clay and I exchanged a quick look and headed towards where the eyes had appeared. Clay moved out of my shadows so we could come at him from two directions. It didn't matter. Glitter, should he still live, could see through my shadows anyways.

We didn't need to worry. We found him sprawled at the back of the abandoned store. My dagger was embedded in his shoulder, and he was bleeding from two bullet wounds. He was still breathing, though it was ragged.

"Stay down, Glitter," I growled, holding my (as of

yet unused) cool taser gun. My finger itched to pull the trigger.

He smiled as he heard my voice. "Dessert…come… save…Glitter?" A tear rolled down his cheek, lit by the strange light in his eyes. I looked down and saw chains on his feet and arms. He'd been held here. And, by the wounds underneath the chains, he had been for a while. The stench emphasized that point.

Make sure all enemies are gone. I looked up, away from Glitter as his breath grew more and more shallow, and glanced toward Clay. I dropped my shadows so he could see me.

"Something's wrong," I said, keeping my voice low.

"No, Tira," he said, smile too wide, eyes too focused. "Something's *very* right."

And he pulled out his gun and fired a volley of bullets my way.

26

I WRAPPED my shadows back around me as I threw myself down, but not quickly enough. A bullet grazed my lower back, just below my armor, searing hot flame shooting through my body. Another struck my left arm, but it didn't feel like it had pierced. Just a flesh wound, I hoped.

I missed my landing completely, crashing hard on my side and getting the wind knocked out of me. Stars exploded in front of my eyes as I rolled away.

Clay screamed and leapt, landing inches from me, blade down. It was hard to imagine he was trying to do anything else but skewer me.

He looked down, spotting my handy trail of blood.

A wicked grin split his lips, and he struck down with his blade, right where I sat. I moved out of the way fast, pushing back and up, landing on my feet and throwing two sleeping darts his way.

He intended to kill me. But I didn't intend to die here.

Not like this, and not at his hands.

The darts hit his neck. He stumbled one step, then he screamed and seemed to regain his energy.

Tradenaline. Oh shit. Of course he'd have some, too. He'd crash damn hard, but it would keep him standing for a while.

I moved, not waiting to see how this was going to resolve itself. I started running back toward the door, pulling shadows around me, but a strong arm grabbed my belt and yanked back so hard I thought I'd be cut in two. I grunted and went flying, scattering my shadows along the way.

Pushing myself back up, I grabbed my shadows again and dove behind an old cracked planter as more bullets flew my way.

I'd be dead before I figured out what the hell was going on.

Glitter cowered on the ground, trying to protect his already-damaged body by curling up in the fetal position. Why the hell was he making Clay attack me? Why was he in chains?

No time to worry about that. I aimed the taser at him, but Clay set off some type of percussion bomb, my head splitting in two as I landed on my knees. It lasted only a (very disorienting) second, but I'd dropped the weapon. And my shadows.

Clay threw a dagger and I stumbled sideways, pulled my shadows to me, the dagger nicking my leg. Not enough to slow me down as I took off running, fairly terrified for my life.

Think, Tira, think! I dashed left, down the corridor,

to reach the second empty store. The metal gate that used to shutter it had long been destroyed, but at least I could get some cover behind the abandoned display cases.

Why would Glitter make him attack me? I took a deep breath, willing my thoughts and heart to slow down. My shadows seemed to be holding, and I couldn't see much of a trail of blood leading to my hiding place. Maybe he'd lose my trail.

Scritch. Boots on glass. Clay had never been stealthy, which was both useful and terrifying right now. I stayed perfectly still, hoping hiding would prove my salvation.

I couldn't take him in hand-to-hand combat. He was way stronger. But I could probably outthink him, especially since he seemed to be under someone's control. Not to mention pumped full of Tradenaline.

Why was Glitter in chains? Unless Glitter wasn't doing this. Sweat trickled down my back.

You've seen this before. I'd been so focused on Glitter that I hadn't seen the obvious. This had happened once before. But not with Glitter.

With the old woman from the Wolf Pack League. The one who'd been nabbed by the same people who had taken Ian.

Lorna.

She was here. And she was using her powers against us. Maybe she didn't know it was us? Maybe she'd freed herself, messed up Glitter and was (justifiably) scared of any intruder?

I realized that I couldn't hear Clay anymore. I

managed to shift a split second before his axe landed directly where I'd been crouching.

Crashing into another display, I pushed hard against it with my legs and toppled it onto Clay. He fell, thrashing, under its weight. It wouldn't keep him down long, but maybe long enough.

"I know it's you, Lorna! We're not here to hurt you!"

I stumbled into the hallway. And there she stood, white hair lit up by a ray of moonlight piercing through the roof. She flicked her hand, and my shadows faded away.

"Clever girl," she smiled. Then something hit me in the back of the head, hard.

I GRUNTED AWAKE, the chain clasped around my ankle clanging. Clay lay like a lump beside me. I reached over, almost crying with relief when I found his pulse.

The cuff around my ankle seemed pretty rudimentary and I reached down to pick it, but it didn't have a lock. I glanced at Clay. He was similarly bound. And these chains weren't just iron, either. Some kind of fancy metal. Probably to resist Traded powers.

I looked around. We were in a store that had been converted into some kind of cell. Other chains hung from the walls and floor, though they (currently) stood empty. The place reeked of old sweat and blood.

Great. Just amazingly great.

There were no bars, but some kind of field shimmered in front of the store.

This sucked.

"Clay," I whispered, and he grunted. "Clay!" I said more forcefully, failing to wake him, but succeeding in making my head hurt. I reached behind my scalp. My fingers came away covered in blood.

This really, really sucked.

I shifted, realizing there was a thin layer of old, dirty hay beneath me. Like they kept us here like animals. A shiver ran down my body. This wasn't good. This wasn't good at all, and no one knew where Clay and I were.

I tried to pull the chain off my ankle, but it wouldn't budge. Tentatively I stood up, but the chain only gave me a few feet of freedom. I couldn't see much. The place was mostly dark, lit only by the strange shimmering field and the moonlight from the corridor.

Footsteps came down that corridor. I reached for my weapons, but of course they were all gone.

Damn it. Why did everyone always take my weapons?

Four people stopped before the shield. Lorna, standing confident with a wicked glint in her eye. Glitter, slumped between two dark-clad guards. His mummy wrappings were askew and covered in blood. His eyes glowed with desperation.

A thousand questions hammered into my head. Smart questions. Insightful ones, even. Yet all that slipped out of my mouth was: "what the hell?"

A fair question, in my defense.

"Because I'm tired of this world, that's why." Lorna said, voice crackling. Clay still didn't move, and I shifted to stand in front of him. I didn't like the hungry look in her eyes.

"You've been doing all of this?" I looked from her to

Glitter, who cast a weary glance my way. I hated him. I'd liked Glitter, once. Like the little brother I'd never had—or wanted, really.

He'd been my friend. I thought so, anyway. And then he'd taken over my mind. And taken Ian away. While I lay there, completely useless, unable to save him.

I hated him, but seeing him slumped, it was clear that some of that attachment still lurked in my heart. Probably because I'd never been taught to deal with my emotions in a constructive manner.

"Oh, don't be mad at Glitter," Lorna said. "I've been playing him like a fiddle since you met him. Poor little mind controllable Traded." She patted his head and he flinched.

"Why would you do that?" I said, hands forming fists at my sides. She'd messed with Glitter. Who'd messed with Ian. It had all been her.

"I already told you," she said, focusing back on me. "I want to go home. I need genetic markers to do that. Traded have them. I was being watched so much that I couldn't steal all the Traded. But sweet, innocent, simple Glitter…well, no one looks twice at the person they'd prefer not be in the room with them." She shrugged and tugged on one of his bandages. I wondered why he was so covered. I'd never asked. Now, I'd probably never find out.

"I'm sorry, Glitter," I whispered.

Glitter started to cast a shy grin my way, but flinched when the old woman spoke up again. "He made for an easy patsy. No one's missed him since he was gone. And people never suspect the old woman. Damn gender biases."

This was getting me nowhere and just seemed to make Glitter melt more. I wasn't sure I trusted him, but I wanted to give him a chance to explain himself. That was a conversation for another day, however. Time to change tactics.

"The Boss was really hurt at having lost you, you know."

"I know," she said, and shrugged. "But she's got her agenda, too. Can't fault me for having my own ambitions."

"You're an agent of the Guild of Shadows?"

"Am I?" she seemed downright amused. I took a step toward her, but couldn't get any further. I really wanted to smack her.

She pulled her barrette free, white hair tumbling down to her waist in light, loose curls. With one swift motion of her wrist, she pricked Glitter with the barrette's sharp edge. He immediately slumped. For half a second I feared the worse, but then he started to snore.

"That's what they give to operatives," I said, looking down at Clay. She ignored me.

"Everyone is sleeping so soundly, except you, Tira," she sounded amused, like she was playing the best game ever.

"Tell you what. I'll give you a choice. Glitter, or Clay," she stretched out their names in a possessive way that made my skin crawl. "I need more material, and one of these two will give it to me."

"…material?" I asked, my hands growing numb, knowing damn well what she was talking about. The steel in her eyes and grin confirmed my fear. Visions of Jorg Loops' bloodied grin crossed my vision before I took a deep, shaky breath and focused.

I stared at Glitter's slumped form, still held up by the two guards. He'd been my friend, once. I thought he'd betrayed me, but he'd just been a pawn under Lorna's control.

Lorna. She'd controlled me, too. Or had both of them been in on it? It didn't matter. I needed to find out more before I condemned Glitter to death. He seemed so helpless. So creepy. But so helpless.

And Clay…*no.* I could never hand her Clay. He'd followed me here to find someone he didn't even like, because it was important to me.

"Choose, or I will," she said casually, like we were talking about cupcake flavors.

The answer came so easily I barely had to think about it.

"Me," I said. "You can have me." It wasn't much of a choice. Not really. I was the only one who was conscious. The only who could witness where they took me. To get a chance to escape. Failing that, Glitter and Clay would survive and hopefully save me.

I swallowed hard as she looked me up and down appraisingly, weighing my worth.

"A noble sacrifice," her voice practically purred. "How exciting!"

I hadn't realized "desperate" and "couldn't live with the alternative" were synonymous with "noble."

"I'd love to know more about how you control shadows," she mused, "similar to mine, but so different...I accept your trade, Tira Misu." She grinned like she was being clever. The shield dropped and several more guards, wearing dark red uniforms, filed in. Lorna came toward me without hesitation.

I wanted to hit her, but she stayed just out of reach. Then she flicked her hand, and shadows wrapped around me, holding my limbs in place. I tried to push against them, but she laughed.

"Not these shadows, Tira. These are mine, and will only obey me." They did seem different. Purple glowed in their depths. Regardless of what that meant, I couldn't get them to budge.

"Yes, you'll do nicely," she whispered, running her fingers down the side of my face, as though analyzing cattle. "Extra material in your horns and tail." I gritted my teeth.

"Who are you?" I whispered, wishing I could fight free, sweat streaming down my face as I struggled against her powers.

"Does it matter?" She sounded amused.

Then she turned, the guards unceremoniously dragged me, and Glitter and Clay, out of the darkened room.

THIS STRIP MALL hadn't seemed that long from the outside. Maybe being dragged while effectively paralyzed just made it seem endless. I'm sure the guards felt the same. I hoped one of them would throw out their back.

I knew I had only one chance to escape. My last dose of Tradenaline. Problem was, I couldn't activate it without a modicum of movement. I couldn't move my arms at all, though I managed to shift my neck a bit to look around, as we entered a large store at the end of the mall. This one had a few lights on, and some hay on sections of the floor, and a large hole in the roof, though it shimmered like the door to the cell had.

Weak sounds caught my attention. Bleating. Meowing. Barking.

Animals?

Why the hell were they gathering all these animals? *Just like when I'd found Ian!* The first time I'd met him in his dog form, he'd been trapped in a room filled with dead animals, chopped to pieces.

The smell struck me, harsh and acrid. My stomach churned as I remembered the fate that could have befallen Ian. Trying to take a deep gulp of air just sent a fouler stench into my lungs. I retched. Well, that had been a long time coming.

"Damn it. She threw up," one of the guards said.

"Poor thing. Maybe her nose is too sensitive for our home," Lorna said. She sounded further away. But not so far that my last dart might not hit her. I just needed to get Tradenaline into me. Then I could take her down. Free the animals. Hopefully find Ian here (in dog form. I liked hugging dogs), and then save Clay and Glitter and get out of here.

Solid plan.

The guards threw me down on the dirty hay, the stench turning my stomach again. A few tools lay nearby, to solidify the cages, no doubt. A particularly interesting looking wrench caught my attention. I really wanted to hit something.

Clay and Glitter were still knocked out. Which really sucked. I couldn't drag them both out. I couldn't abandon them. Or, at least, not Clay. I was still struggling with the Glitter reveal.

I really wanted to be anywhere else but here. Somewhere safe, with the few people I cared about fine and alive, and laughing…damn it. This wasn't helping me, and the stench of rotten hay squashed that fantasy pretty fast. This situation sucked so bad.

But maybe I could still do something. Anything would be better than nothing.

I took a deep breath, focusing on the movement around me. Lorna was distracted, instructing the guards nearby. Hopefully she wasn't aware of the Tradenaline. It had been a more recent development in the Traded world. And she probably thought I only kept sleeping darts in my Guild of Shadows barrette, which I used as a belt buckle.

I liked those trusty sleeping darts, which is why I also kept a few in my wrist guard.

I strained hard against Lorna's shadows, and felt giddy with anticipation as my fingers twitched. Lorna's hold must have weakened with her attention diverted elsewhere. Careful not to move quickly enough for them to spot me, I painstakingly moved my hand. With enormous effort, I was eventually able to move my arm, though it wasn't super graceful. I just needed to reach my sigil and…a beep. The needle thrust into me. My back arched and I gasped. The Tradenaline shot through my body.

I pulled out the dart and rolled right, spotting the white hair and throwing it before anyone could react. She grunted and reached for her neck, the remaining (super weird) shadows tumbling away from me as I gathered my (much better) shadows and vanished. I didn't stick around to watch her fall, pushing myself towards that wrench, trying hard not to think of Clay lying there, helpless.

The guards screamed, two mean-looking jacked-up

fighters covered completely in red. They had a lot of weapons.

But I had a wrench.

I found the first cage, smashed the lock and threw the door open. A bunch of goats spilled out and scattered towards the entrance. I headed to the next cage and freed a bunch of…monkeys, maybe? I'd never seen a monkey.

"She's letting the animals escape!" one of the guards cried. He looked like he was wavering between shooting them and letting them go.

"Grab them alive, you idiots!" Lorna muttered, her voice weak.

Good.

I freed three more cages, two filled with puppies, but no Ian. My heart lurched. Dogs raced out, most running straight for the exit, seizing their chance at freedom. Some were terrified, cowering in the corner. And I didn't have the time to coax them out. But I could buy them time to maybe find the motivation to move.

Ducking past another cage, I freed a bunch of angry cats, the guards screaming as they tried to catch them (dogs were great friends, but cats were great weapons). There were only two cages left.

The Tradenaline was turning me loopy, making it hard to keep my shadows tight around me, especially since the whole space had suddenly flooded with light. Above me, wind picked up, and a helicopter hovered into the large space.

"That's not safe," I mumbled, as a column of water crashed into me. I choked, seconds before electricity coursed through the water. My whole body spasmed as the current hit me, knocking the breath out of me. Even Tradenaline couldn't fight the shock and pain, and I collapsed to my knees, my shadows deserting me. My hair stuck to my numb face as I fought to take in a breath.

Two legs appeared before me. Two old, mean legs. Lorna grabbed the back of my hair and pulled, forcing me to look up at her. "That's quite enough," she said, as though speaking to a naughty pet. "I hope you enjoyed your finale."

I spotted the last few dogs slipping out of the door, choosing escape over facing the terrible helicopter monster. Couldn't blame them. Part of me felt that I'd managed to save Ian, at least in spirit.

Overall, this wasn't too bad a finale.

HANDS PUSHED me down on something hard. I tried to put up a fight, but between the Tradenaline crash and the electric shock, I mostly just gurgled. My hands and legs were strapped down.

I didn't like this one bit.

Lorna suddenly stood over me, spending an uncomfortable amount of time staring at my horns.

"The other two are in a cage," one of the guards said.

"You promised you wouldn't hurt them," I managed to mumble.

"I won't," she said, scraping my horn with a scalpel. It didn't hurt, but sent a shiver down my spine. She took the dark flake and brought it to her microscope.

"You don't have to do this," I said, testing the bonds. The effort made me woozy, the room spinning and I had to close my eyes and gulp in deep breaths.

"I do, I'm afraid," she said, head still turned. I continued gulping breaths, wishing my head would stop spinning. I really sucked at Tradenaline. "There's no other way, Tira. I tried using materials from creatures of this world, but it just doesn't work."

The animals. From the room. Where I'd found Ian. Maybe she'd been experimenting on them, first? Before I could find a way to voice the question and clear my head, she was right beside me. My eyes snapped open. Old eyes peered at me.

"It's too bad that shock didn't knock you out," she said. "This would be a lot more pleasant for you."

She vanished behind me. I struggled against the bonds, but they wouldn't budge. A strap was tightened around my forehead. Fear turned my thoughts to lead. Then a sound.

A chainsaw?

Pain exploded down my spine, stars slammed my sight. A thousand daggers jabbed my neck and reached every bone, my head vibrating with pain so intense I couldn't think enough to try to stop my screams, which I could barely hear over the sound of the chainsaw. Which must have been cutting my skull in two, it was so loud, rattling my brain to mush. Cold sweat broke out across my entire body and bile splashed my tongue.

The world was pain, and I think I might have passed out for a few seconds, but not much. The sound ended. But the world still vibrated. I gulped in air, acid in my throat, my hand closing and opening like a broken vice.

I blinked away the hot tears and I could see again, though everything was shaky.

"What an amazing piece of biology," Lorna

muttered as she placed the half of my horn she'd just shorn off, under the microscope. Warming blood pooled on my head where it dribbled freely from my horn, or ex-horn, I suppose. I tried damn hard not to lose consciousness at the sight of my own body part being coldly examined.

Without meaning to, I moaned. A guttural sound I wasn't proud of, but damn, that hurt. Everything hurt. Like a spike had been jabbed in my head, every nerve ending on fire.

"Now now, don't fuss," Lorna cooed as she placed my horn in a sample bag. "It's not personal."

"It feels personal," I said, looking at my horn. I'd hated my horns. I should be glad one of them was gone. I'd look more human. But I already felt like a piece of me was missing.

Which, I suppose, it really was. I started to giggle. Blood loss and Tradenaline crash, combined with the pure trauma of having a piece of me sawed off claimed their toll.

Oh well, at least I'll die laughing.

The pain spliced my head again, and nothing seemed funny anymore. I almost passed out, eyes rolling back in my head. I fought to stay awake.

"The Guild of Shadows is gone," I whispered, in case she cared. "I don't have a home anymore." I hadn't meant to say that last part out loud, surprising myself with my own words. Everything hurt even more.

Lorna stopped examining my horn and came over to me, looking down at me as though seeing me for the first time.

"You have a home, child," she said, voice soft, like we were the only two people in the world. "A home faraway, with parents who probably still want you. Just like the humans here still want their children back, Tira. And that's all I'm trying to do. Get us home."

"I'll be dead," I said, feeling the blood from my horn pooling behind my head. Those things bled a lot, turned out.

"Possibly," she said. "But somewhere in each of us lies the answer to where among the stars we belong, Tira."

"Why the animals?" I asked. Maybe if I kept her talking, she'd stop sawing.

"Because I needed baseline comparisons from this world to ours. Better animals than people, I figured."

Her attention drifted as she looked up at my horn, then down, as though deciding what else she could saw off.

"Where's Ian?" I asked, testing my bonds. No luck.

"Don't worry about him, child. We all have our own journey," she shushed me, then looked down. "Your tail might also give some fascinating insight. I've only studied a few Traded with tails. It'll hurt though. But, if you're lucky, it's fused to your spine, and you should lose all feeling once we cut enough nerves."

I moaned, the pain in my head unrelenting. That didn't sound lucky. I hadn't liked my tail, either. It made it hard to sit in chairs, and it moved when I didn't want it to. But I didn't want to lose it, either.

"I'm a demon girl," I slurred as the table moved,

shifting me up so she could look at my tail. "Don't take my tail."

"You're not a demon. None of the Traded are. We're all just from different worlds. Different species which humans named based on their limited understanding of the cosmos."

I felt her pull on my tail, hard, as it snapped into something, keeping it straight and extended. "Please don't do this," I said, my voice lacking any courage. I was done with courage. I'd just wanted to find my friend.

"We're all from different worlds, but your generation is the strangest. You don't have some of the markers of the older ones. Portal markers, I think. A genetic flaw that made every one of us a worthy target."

She tsk'd. "I'm not sure this is tied directly to your spine. You might have a separate spinal junction in your lower back. Gives you more mobility and flexibility, I suppose. Impressive. You should learn to make better use of it, Tira," she paused and broke out into laughter. "Oh, wait. You won't have it much longer, so it doesn't matter!"

Still laughing, she headed behind me. Now that she'd placed me in a more vertical position, blood streamed down my face. My horns didn't clot quickly, apparently. Or the overuse of Tradenaline had thinned out my blood.

Passing out from the blood loss might be a blessing.

"No, your generation is useful for investigating which markers are different in us. Like with your friend, Ian."

"Ian," I repeated, trying to snap my eyes open, but the world around me was too heavy.

"He'll be sad you're dead," Lorna said, stepping to my right to her chainsaw, still slick with my blood. A sob caught in my throat. Ian was still alive, and I was going to die before him. Then who would try to save him?

"I believe I'll bring him a souvenir," she stepped beside me, holding my horn like it was the greatest joke in the world. Imagining Ian giving up what fight he had left, imagining him finally killed after holding out so long for *me* to come save him...

I snapped and screamed, trying to break free. My screams echoed through the room, and I called every shadow around me, urging them not to protect me, but to hit her. To destroy her. To pick her up and throw her against the wall.

They came, out of every corner. The darkness thickened, an odd odor of smoke permeating the space, cleansing it. Lorna blinked, uncertain what was happening. She held out her hand defensively, her own strange shadows rising to protect her.

But she was too late, and I was too angry. My shadows slammed into her, pushing her back.

My shadows are not just lack of light, I remembered the feeling of making them opaque. Of bringing them out of the spectrum of light into that of solid objects. Sweat streamed down my face, or maybe it was just blood, and I began to feel lightheaded, my grasp on the shadows vanishing.

And then, Lorna took hold of them, laughing. "Oh,

Tira, we could have been friends." Her smile vanished and her haunted eyes held mine captive. "If you survive this, I promise I will see you home, child. Someday, you'll thank me for what I did this day."

And then the shadows slammed into me, knocking the wind out of me.

Darkness. A flash of light. Pain. A scream—maybe my own. My head fell forward uselessly. I think I passed out.

More screaming. Shouting. A pair of strong arms wrapping around me. Someone pressing something against my horn. It hurt so bad I screamed and tried to push them away.

"Tira, it's Clay. You're okay. Don't fight us."

And the fight melted out of me and into the darkness. And I melted into Clay.

30

I drifted on the edge of consciousness, flooding me with aches and memories I'd much rather forget. But the pain in my head begged attention, and I grunted and shifted, reaching for my horn.

"Don't touch it," Clay said, the bed buckling beside me as he sat down. "It's healing, but it's best not to touch it."

"Okay," I said, struggling to open my eyes, I was so groggy.

I started drifting again when Clay spoke up, like he couldn't quite stand the silence. "I'm glad you're okay."

"I'm glad you're okay, too," I mumbled, forcing my eyes to open. I focused on him, dark eyes filled with concern and questions. Nicks and scars marred his face. "Glitter?"

"In the infirmary. Regenerates well, though, so he'll be fine. Just needs a bit more time."f

"Good," I remembered him growing a whole leg back at one point. Gross, but useful. And I didn't want him dead. Not if he'd been used like Lorna. She'd hurt him, too.

"How did we get out?"

He grinned. I loved that grin. "The Wolf Pack League came to get us," he said, looking proud.

"How did they find us?" I struggled to sit up, and he helped me, gently leaning me against the wall, his leg against mine. He handed me some water, which I gratefully drank, washing away the bitter taste lingering in my mouth.

"They tracked me via my smart phone," he shrugged, like it was no big deal. The glass sat forgotten in my hand as I stared at him.

"You didn't disable it?" I had with mine. First thing. I'd blocked any way I thought they might be able to track me. Because you never knew.

Especially when you were being hunted. I'd offered to help Clay disable his, but he'd said it was fine. He had it.

"Clay, that could have gotten us killed."

"It didn't, though. It got us saved." He hesitated, then pushed through, "look, I trust these people with my life. Like I trust you, Tira. You should stay here. With the Guild of Shadows gone, you should be able to, now!"

He wanted me to be here with him so badly. And I wanted to stay, too. To be with the one friend I could trust. The one person who cared for me, still.

But I couldn't. Blake wanted to hurt me. And Ian still needed me.

"I can't," I said, feeling numb.

"If it's because of the Watch," he said, voice patient. He'd rehearsed this, getting ready for my objections, "they don't have as much power over us, apparently." Did I imagine the pride in his voice?

"Boss said she'll negotiate something. She wants to talk to you when you feel better." I nodded, the numbness creeping into my toes. I gathered my knees up and hugged them, leaning my head on them, horn throbbing dully. "Then, we'll figure stuff out and get Ian back. If that's still what you want." He shot me a joking grin, making sure I knew he didn't mean that last part. Well, didn't mean it fully, anyway.

"I wish I had your strength to fight this world all the time, Clay," I whispered, turning toward him. "I just don't."

"You're plenty strong," he said, hand covering mine. "You've just had a bad go of it, that's all."

"I wish everything was easier, you know?" I said, looking toward him. His dark eyes focused on me, sending a shiver down my spine. With Clay, I felt completely seen. And completely accepted.

"So do I," he leaned in, his lips finding mine, his hand weaving in my hair and crushing me to him, deepening his kiss. I leaned into him, wanting nothing more than to melt into him, to hold him until I forgot about the world...*Ian*. I pulled away with a jerk, guilt stabbing my heart.

Clay looked disappointed, but he shifted back, gently letting me go. Just like I'd been afraid I was letting go of Ian, just moments ago. Which was ridiculous.

And yet… "I'm sorry," I said.

"Don't be," he insisted, eager to break the awkwardness settling between us. "You're great as you are." He gave a quick laugh. "I, um, I guess I miss you, like, a lot. But I don't want to ever make you uncomfortable."

I smiled at him. I loved him so much. But I couldn't just lose myself in him. Out of fear, guilt, worry…I just wasn't sure anymore. Why were emotions so damn hard?

"I miss you, too," I said, meaning it. "And you don't make me uncomfortable." I leaned in and gently kissed his cheek.

For a second he looked relieved, than sadness washed over him, his eyes lowering.

"Clay?" I said, putting my arm on his, wanting to dispel his obvious pain.

Clay looked like he wanted to say something, but then his hands curled into fists, and with a deep breath found his resolve again. "We should go," he said softly. "The Boss is waiting."

And, just like that, Clay shut me out of his pain, and I had no clue how to bridge this new gap between us.

31

"Just you for now," Sam told Clay, looking at me apologetically.

"I get it," I said. "Official league business and all that good stuff."

"I won't be long," he said, squeezing my hand and walking into the Boss' office. Or throne room. Whatever.

To help the time pass, I decided to analyze the space again, even though I knew it pretty well. This whole place was so weird. The top floors were almost medieval-looking, full of flagstone walls. This lower floor was decorated like an old office building. Beige and yellow everything, faded, lined wallpaper, desks that had stood the test of time but certainly not of style.

I pushed back my hair, annoyed that it kept slipping into my face. I hadn't realized my horn had done so much to hold it back. Maybe I'd actually have to start using my barrette, which annoyed me even more.

I never thought I'd miss my horn. My tail whished,

signaling my annoyance. I automatically went to stop it.

Why? They'd almost taken that, too. No one would ever see me as anything more than the demon I was, so why fight so much against it? I felt naked for having lost half a horn, a mark of my demonhood, or whatever the hell I was. How would I feel if I'd have lost my tail?

Slowly, methodically, I let my tail do its thing. Damn, that was uncomfortable. But I thought I could get used to it. Or at least accept it.

Demon girl. That's what Blake always called me. That's what Lorna had called me as she'd sawed my horn off, even as she went on about humans and their limited terminology. I could still feel the saw biting into it, resonating through my skull and down my spine, stars exploding before my eyes…my hair slipped in front of my eyes and I pushed it back again, grateful for the distraction, if not the reminder, of the missing horn.

"Need some help with that?" Jolene said, voice like warm apple cider. I almost automatically said no, I was fine. But her blond hair was always perfectly styled. No one had ever taught me how to put up my hair, and going into battle without something holding it back seemed like a bad idea.

"Please," I said, and she quickly hid her surprise with a smile. She sat me in a side office and pulled out her purse, which apparently held an entire beauty salon. Spotting my surprised glance at how much stuff she was pulling out of there, she gave an awkward laugh.

"I know. I'm vain. I'm okay with it."

"That's not it," I said, "you just get so much in there! It's impressive!"

"I suppose it is," she laughed under her breath.

"And it's okay to be vain," I said, looking at her. "You're beautiful, and it makes anyone looking at you happy."

She looked stunned for half a second, then smiled broadly. "Thank you, sugar plum. You know, you're every bit as sweet as Clay says you are."

I flushed slightly, then gave a laugh. "You know, flushing always bothered me. I thought it made my purple skin too visible." I looked down at my purple hands on my lap. "But when she cut my horn away, even though I'd always wanted them gone, I realized it wouldn't change who and what I was," I sighed, blaming the Tradenaline crash for my sudden openness with Jolene. I pushed forward, voice barely audible, even to me.

"The world might always see me as a demon, but I don't have to."

Jolene enveloped me in a giant hug from behind. "Oh, sugar, the world sucks. This one, anyway. You're amazing. Don't let anyone tell you different. And you don't hug!" she quickly let go. "Oh my dear, I'm sorry."

"I don't mind your hugs," I said, smiling at her. She wasn't awkward like Clay and me. With her, it felt different. "You're like a cozy blanket."

She looked perplexed, but decided it was a compliment and just smiled, pulling brushes and elastics from her bag. "Okay, let me look at this…let me know if this hurts, okay?"

I braced myself. Jolene pulled off the bandage, which stung a little bit. "It's healed up nicely," she said. "We sealed it with some tar, of all things. But it just wouldn't stop bleeding."

"That's pretty smart," I said.

"My idea," she grinned. "The old traitorous woman got away with your horn," that was as much venom as I'd ever heard in Jolene's voice, and even then it wasn't much, "but if we get it back, I think we might be able to actually glue it back on. If that's what you want."

"Okay. I'm not sure." I frowned, looking ahead, not wanting to make a sudden move as she started gently brushing my hair. No one else had ever brushed my hair, and I suddenly understood why dogs liked pats.

"That's okay," she said. "But you think on it, and if the opportunity comes up, you let me know then, okay?"

"Okay," I said, though I wasn't sure that there was much to think about. It was a part of me. A part that had been taken by force. Reclaiming it would probably feel good, right?

Jolene hummed as she braided my hair, taking the time to explain to me how she did it, and what I could do differently. In between explanations, I let my mind drift—to where I'd been, and where I was.

How it seemed easier to fit in here, to be one of the Wolf Pack League. Not because it's where I felt I belonged, but because Clay had vetted everyone here. They were *his* friends, so I didn't have to worry about betrayal or ill intent. Because I trusted him more than myself, apparently, at least when it came to judging people.

But he'd been wrong about Ian. Ian was good people. And Rachel had been great, too. Even Gorsel had had redeeming qualities. And Jombo had seemed to care. And no one had ever called me demon girl there. No one had judged me for wanting to hide in my shadows. I'd just been so afraid they might, that I'd anticipated they would.

Damn it. They were gone. They were all gone. And released from my responsibilities to the Guild, I didn't think I was going to get to choose where to go next. No more so than before. That loss was much worse than my horn.

Maybe I could still help some of them. Maybe, if I gave myself up, I could plead for latitude.

I doubted it. This world was nothing if not unkind. But I *had* to try. At the least, I had to find a way to get them the information about Ian. So they could finish what I couldn't.

"Tira, Clay's topped off in his categories," Jolene said, thankfully stopping my tailspin. She was almost done the braid, which kept the hair nicely tucked against my head and out of my face. She'd left the other side loose, and I liked the asymmetry, though it would take some getting used to.

"I know," I said. "He's really good."

"He is," she agreed, securing the braid with an elastic as I watched with her handheld mirror. "Every fighter has to go up when they've topped, Tira. Clay's fighting against it because you asked him to, and the Boss is putting up with it because he's worth it, but that won't last."

I looked back at her in the mirror. She met my eyes, then looked away, embarrassed. "How useful is a fighter who won't fight to his full potential?"

"That could get him killed," I shot back.

"It could," she said, "and so could your missions at the Guild of Shadows." She sighed as I reeled. "Look, he's respecting your choice to stay at the Guild."

She didn't know the Guild of Shadows was gone. That made me feel a bit better, somehow. Like Clay had known I'd want privacy.

When I didn't respond, she pushed forward. "You owe it to him to respect his choice, too."

"Some choice," I mumbled, not sure if I was referring to his, or mine. "Thanks for the braid," I said as I stood, "I'm going to see if they're done now."

"Okay, sugar," she said, not pushing her point any further. She didn't need to. She knew I'd heard, even though I really didn't want to.

She knew that I understood. Sure, the Guild of Shadows had its issues, but I (mostly) knew what they were. It had been my home. And though the Wolf Pack League seemed warmer on the outside, inside it was just as cold and deadly as the rest of the Traded world.

HERDED TOWARD THE BATTLE ARENA, I spotted the Boss gazing contentedly over it, even though it was only a practice battle. I recognized Clay's grunts and peeked over the fence. He was going against Sam, who was giving him tricks on using the slippery terrain to his advantage.

Clay spotted me and waved. I waved back, and winced as he took a blow while his attention was diverted.

"Stay focused!" Sam hollered, and I couldn't agree more. Clay laughed and went back on the offensive. He was having a field day. My heart missed a beat, glad he was back to his usual self.

I turned my attention to the Boss, hating how she scrutinized the fight below. I could almost see dollar signs streaming before her eyes.

"Operative Misu," her gravel voice beckoned. I headed her way and stood near her, but kept my eyes trained on the battle below. If she wasn't going to give me her full attention, I hardly saw the point of giving her mine.

"I find myself in an awkward position," she said, gesturing below. "A fighter who doesn't want to go up in the ranks because the girl he loves tells him not to."

I flushed bright purple and tried to sputter out a protest, but she held up her hand.

"Traded. Emotionally stunted aliens from another world," she sighed. "It doesn't matter. The problem is that I have to justify every Traded's existence here, and I can only do that if they're fighting to their full potential."

The implication wasn't lost on me.

"I believe in a fair exchange," she said, swirling a pearlescent drink in her hand. "You let Clay go, and I'll help you get Ian back. I believe they're both competing for your heart?"

More sputtering. I didn't know what bothered me more: that she so easily stated the things I hadn't even begun to understand, or that she'd figured it all out so easily, without even really spending time with me.

"Well?" she said. "I'll get my fighters to help you find your missing dog, and you two can live happily ever after."

There was a grunt below and Clay burst into laughter. He was having so much fun. He loved the arena. Loved the glory.

I can't keep you safe, I realized, sorrow making the world a bit dimmer. But I could encourage him to be as safe as possible. By cheering him on. By working out strategies. I really believed that Clay could be one of their best fighters. But not if I held him back.

Especially not if I held him back. Because it was clear to me that he'd be forced to move forward. And he'd fight against it, getting himself killed trying to follow my request.

Either way, he was going to be facing those matches. With or without me. Wouldn't it be better if he felt he could tell me anything, still?

"No," I whispered, "I'll not barter one friend's life for another."

"No?" she asked, turning to finally look at me. "And what if that would seal your entrance into the Wolf Pack League? Clay informed me of your troubles with the Watch. They won't interfere with us as they would with the Guild of Shadows. What if, instead, I make sure you get to stay here. With him." She gestured toward Clay, who still battled below. I followed her movement, my heart beating a bit faster at the sight of him.

She turned back to look at the battle, her voice distant when she spoke again. "I could probably force your hand, you know. Make you forget Ian, and stay here with Clay. Care for him when he gets injured." A pause. "Give him a reason to survive those battles."

I wanted to close my eyes and be anywhere else but here. To get lost in my shadows. But I was alone in my shadows, and I wanted my friends safe. I didn't want to be hunted by the Watch, or forced to stay at the League, I realized. I wanted to go back to the Guild of Shadows.

Home.

Sonsil's voice resonated in my head. *Pay attention, Tira. Not everything is as it seems.*

I turned to face her. "You *could* force me, but you gave me a choice, instead," I said, my thoughts forming around my words.

"I'm quite humane that way," she said, taking a practically non-existent sip from her drink.

I snorted. "No, you're not. So, I'm guessing you're just working some sick angle to use against Clay and I."

Her left eyebrow rose slightly.

"Either I've already secured my position here," I said, finding surer footing. "Or you already know you're going to have to help me. Either way, there's only the illusion of choice. Because it's easier to control us when we think we've made a choice, even when there's no choice at all."

She tipped her head sideways, catching me out of the corner of her eye, her lip turned up in amusement. "Ah, see, now that's the kind of thinking I expect from an operative of the Guild of Shadows." She swirled her drink. "Now, tell me, Operative Misu," that was the second time she'd used my title, which struck me as weird, "if I'm willing to lie to pull your strings, don't you think others might do the same?"

Her words struck me like a ton of bricks, blood pounding into my horn.

Blake.

"The Guild of Shadows isn't destroyed," I whispered. "My friend isn't dead."

"It amazes me how smart and how stupid you can be at once, I must say," I didn't even care to protest, my heart leaping in my chest, relief making my limbs numb. "But the Watch did not destroy the Guild, no. That Blake fellow might be overreaching his authority, though no one seems to be stopping him," she leaned toward me, like she was about to give me a great confidence. "It's good to let Traded make their own mistakes and stretch their wings on their own terms. He would, however, like to destroy you." She glanced down at Clay, narrowing her eyes. "I wonder if they'd thank me if I handed you to them."

"You're messing with me again," I said, my tail twitching in annoyance, which turned out to be satisfying this time. "You can't afford a war with the Guild of Shadows."

Saying that name felt sweet. Like I belonged to something. I really hoped emotions wouldn't get the best of me. Not in front of her. Not now. "And you're not in a position to bargain."

I held up my hand to stop her protest. To my surprise, she held her peace. "It was your operative who kidnapped our second-in-command. And did this to me," I pointed to my horn. She didn't look up, knowing full well what had been done.

"But, I'd be dead if your league hadn't helped." Her features darkened a bit. So she hadn't given her blessing for that particular mission. "So we'll call it even."

She snorted and took a sip of her drink.

"So, how do you want to proceed from here?" I said, amazed at how far she'd let me push her and wondering when she'd push back.

"I don't want the Guild of Shadows involved," she said immediately. There was the push back. "Quite frankly, I don't trust your guild."

"Fair enough," I said. "I doubt my guild trusts you, either. But we're good at finding leads and exploring. You're good at hitting things. Seems we could use each other."

She narrowed her eyes. "Not yet," she said. "My main problem, if I'm honest, is you."

I doubted she was being honest, but I waited her out.

"You left your guild. How do you know they won't just arrest you? Hand you over to the Watch? Something they can very easily do. And probably should, if they have any sense of preservation."

Whatever upper hand I'd felt earlier, it was long gone. She knew everything. About how I'd left the Guild. They still survived, sure, but that didn't mean they were rooting for me right now. My stomach flopped. I was getting really tired of these shifting emotions. And I hated that the Boss knew I had nowhere to go, and no leg to stand on.

"I want Lorna," she hissed. "She betrayed me, and I want her to pay. You're an operative from the Guild of Shadows, and you'll help me find her so I can get her. Once that's done, I will personally appeal on your behalf with your leader." Her features soured at the very prospect of helping me out, or of asking for help.

"This sucks," I said, turning back to look down at Clay, crossing my arms. I had no choice, except to take the chance that the Guild would let me stroll back in without stopping me. Not likely.

"It certainly does," the Boss agreed.

I let my tail swish in full annoyance, part of me hoping I'd knock down her damn glass.

3 3

THE OVERLAPPING LOCATIONS between Aia and Blake were the only remaining leads, so we targeted the nearest one. As far as I could tell, there was no real activity worth noting. But, unlike most of the others, this one hadn't been bought and abandoned by a shell company. This one had been built in the middle of the city's large central park. Not a tourist attraction, either.

By the time our minibus (real subtle) pulled up, I vibrated with anticipation. To find Ian. To go back to the Guild of Shadows. To put the pieces of my (sort of) life back together.

The rest of the very well-armed Wolf Pack League stepped off the bus. Once in the cool night air, Clay pulled me aside, warm hand on my arm.

"Tira," he turned to me, shifting his feet, "look, maybe it would be best if you just stay here."

I gave a low laugh. "Clay, no offense to your league, but I'm the only one with good infiltration experience here. You need me."

He shrugged, trying to make light of his words, which only served to annoy me. "I know, but maybe…I mean, what if…shit, Tira, what if we walk in there and find him dead?"

"No!" I snapped at him, the word like a gunshot in the air. So much for selling my infiltration experience.

He held his hands up defensively. "I'm just saying, Tira. It's possible. You don't need to see that. I mean, what I saw down there while you faced Blake…it wasn't good."

"No," I said again, making it clear I wasn't even considering this. "I gave up everything to figure this out to the end. Even if he is dead," I took a deep breath of cold air, "I need to know. To see it for myself, Clay. Otherwise, I'll always have that doubt."

I knew he was just trying to look out for me, but no. I couldn't *not* go. No more than he couldn't go into the death combats.

Damn it. I hated just about everything in this world right now. I closed my eyes to take a deep breath and focus back on the mission at hand. Clay misinterpreted my worry.

"Tira, what did the Boss say?" There hadn't been time to tell him everything. As soon as the mission was approved, we'd moved quickly. I hadn't even had a chance to see Glitter. Which was okay. I wasn't sure I was ready for that, yet.

And I was so glad the Guild of Shadows was fine, but didn't think Clay would be as happy. He'd been light-hearted as we prepped, sprinkling in jokes and laughter, like he thought I'd get to stay.

"She said," I said softly, "that Blake is an even bigger douchebag than we thought."

It took him a second, his amusement at Blake's expense vanishing to leave him crestfallen, though he tried to hide it. "Oh. Your guild is okay."

I nodded, letting the silence sit between us.

"Is it shitty of me to say I'm not that glad?"

I didn't know what to say, so I gently squeezed his arm. He tried to grin at me, but his heart wasn't in it, his eyes betraying the depth of his emotions.

"Let's go beat on something," I suggested.

"Hell yeah," he said, and seemed to perk up a bit. I still felt like shit as I followed him, though. It was damned annoying. I should be happy about my guild! But I cared about Clay and his feelings. I guess there was no winning this one.

Clay, Sam, Sarah (I didn't know her but she had super cool green lipstick on) and I moved forward, my shadows wrapped around them. The rest of the team took cover, waiting in case we needed backup.

We cleared a small park and woods, to reach our destination. A dark structure rose in front of us, hidden by vines and trees. According to Aia's and Blake's notes, there were rumors of people going missing in it, of screams escaping it at night. Those were probably urban legends, since I'm sure it had excellent soundproofing.

We pushed the vines aside, me and the four fighters hidden in my shadows.

"How do we get in?" Sam asked, looking impatiently at the dark, impenetrable circular structure. Its circumference was ten feet, max, so I guessed it led to an underground facility. Always popular with people doing shitty things.

"We break the door down," Clay shrugged.

"There's no door," I pointed out usefully. Another shrug.

"We make a door?"

"I can do that!" Sarah exclaimed, pulling out a pack.

This was going to go bad real quick.

"We have to be quiet!" I said, but she was pulling out a laser cutter, not some explosive device.

"Oh," I said, "okay."

A few minutes and an alarming amount of shadow-testing sparks later, and we were in. The interior revealed a platform with stairs leading down. I gestured for them to stay close, but I wasn't sure they understood. I could feel the adrenaline pumping from them as they prepped for battle.

Infiltration wasn't their guild's thing. They seemed more intent on finding something to punch.

This was definitely not going to go well.

The metal stairs creaked as they took them, like they'd never heard of stealth. A couple of them already looked hyped up on Tradenaline. Seemed pretty early to take the stuff, but Clay shrugged and grinned, looking as excited as the rest of his team. Well, at least he seemed to have gotten over his disappointment over my guild's survival. That was something, I guess.

I wasn't overly surprised when two guards shouted from the awaiting darkness: "Who goes there!"

No shit, we were spotted. Might as well have

screamed out that we were here. Before any of the guards could make any more noise, I let loose two daggers, downing them silently. I'd much prefer the sleeping darts, but I was fresh out of those, and could only replenish at the Guild of Shadows.

"Don't hoard all the fun," Sam reprimanded me.

"Don't make noise," I mouthed back. We reached the bottom, giving our eyes a few more seconds to adjust to the darkness. The two guards had been alone in the small room. A single door stood between their crumpled bodies.

Clay and I positioned ourselves on one side, and Sam and Sarah on the other. Cautiously, we tried the door. Unlocked. Gently, I pushed the door open.

The stench almost knocked all of us down.

"What the hell…" Sarah muttered as we stepped in, my shadows easily pulled around us in the dimness.

Not that it mattered. There was no one alive here to stop us. Two rows of cold metal tables led down the room, buttressed by equipment, vials, and large jars.

Sam leaned over and threw up. I ignored him and kept walking down the rows, looking at each of the tables carefully. I made sure my shadows stayed up, not because I feared detection, but more as a shield against my own growing fears.

Clay stayed near me, within my shadows, but he said nothing. I didn't dare look at him. I just focused on what needed to be done.

And the bodies on the tables. Or, rather, what remained of them. Eyes stared up without seeing, for those who still had eyes. Some had had their organs removed. Others, limbs. Some were missing their entire faces.

That could be me, my heart leapt into my throat. They'd taken my horn, but they could have taken so much more.

I went from table to table, trying to identify bodies. Trying to identify *one* body—Ian.

My feet dragged, warring between my desire to move faster and wanting to turn around and never come back. I pushed forward and started down the second row and still didn't find Ian.

Then I moved back past the first row, looking more closely for anything familiar. There were a few that I thought were from Aia's pictures. I'd have to compare later.

"They deserve to be identified," I whispered. "They might have had a home."

Clay placed a hand on my shoulder, his warmth comforting. "It's not something we can do, Tira. We've got to let this go and head to the next location."

"Blake had been here," I said, feeling numb. "He knew what was happening. And he did nothing to stop it."

"These bodies have been gone for a while, Tira. Blake might have come after the fact."

"Oh," I said, wondering if the two guards were from the Watch.

"But there's no way to know. Either way, he's a shithead."

"A douchebag," I said, without much conviction.

"Come on. We have to go," he said. I nodded and

turned, dropping my shadows. Then I saw it, on the edge of one of the tubes arrayed along the wall. *Infinity Inc.* The same corporation that had bought out Lorna's mall.

But they hadn't bought this out. They'd *supplied* it. If I could find their headquarters…blood pumped through my veins.

I just had to find the corporation's headquarters. There didn't seem to be a trace of them anywhere. I'd been over everything so often. I needed better intel, and that wasn't something I'd find at the Wolf Pack League.

"No," I said, standing my ground. Clay turned back, but he didn't look surprised. "I know who can help clean this up and get these Traded home," I said. The people who kept the peace between Traded and humans. Who stayed in the shadows.

"Tira…" Clay said, but I shook my head.

"Clay, the Boss was right. At some point, I'll have to face them." I gathered my shadows around us, blocking us from the others, though they seemed more interested in staying as far away from the bodies as possible.

"I need to save him, Clay, no matter the cost," I whispered, cupping his cheek in my hand. "You know I love you, right? You'll always be my best friend. But I need to do this."

He took a deep breath and leaned into my hand.

"I get that," he said, and gave me a gentle kiss on the lips. Not the passionate embrace from earlier in his room. "But let me stay with you."

"Okay," I said, not sure I could have said no. Clay held my shoulders and I thought he'd pull me in for a deeper kiss, but he took a deep breath and let go, turning to walk out of my shadows.

I watched him walk away, feeling strangely breathless. Then I dropped my shadows and re-enabled gaublet.

3 4

Sonsil had certainly mastered the art of throwing daggers with a single glance. He'd mostly reserved them for Clay, but I got a few, too. He walked around the room, examining each body as I had done, while other operatives began tagging and bagging.

I stayed to the side with Clay. When Sonsil wanted to talk to me, he'd make it clear.

"Is he always that intense?" Clay muttered.

I nodded, not wanting to be overheard by Sonsil.

Rachel walked in, and I started to feel better instantly. She walked toward me and gathered me in an unexpected hug. I hugged her back, grateful she seemed alright.

"Sorry about almost killing you," she said, though her words revealed the pain she felt at having been under Glitt...I mean, Lorna's control. Clay shifted uncomfortably beside me. I hoped he wasn't too embarrassed. I mean, we'd all been there. I shifted the conversation away from the uncomfortable topic of being turned into a puppet.

"Sorry about destroying your frame," I shrugged back.

"I'm just glad you're alright."

"Me, too," I said, meaning it so much. She smiled and hugged me again, then headed in to help the others.

"She seems nice," Clay said, and I almost rolled my eyes. Oh, sure, a walking explosion seemed nicer than a puppy. *Because he doesn't see her as competition.*

The Boss' words washed over me again and I flushed, my tail twitching behind me. Clay moved back a bit to avoid being hit.

Smart.

I was starting to like my tail a hell of a lot.

Sonsil was done his walkaround and he turned to focus on Clay and me, hands behind his back as he walked toward us. Clay stood straighter, intimidated by the leader of the Guild of Shadows. Which, I couldn't blame him. Sonsil's eyes were so sharp they could cut you if he wanted to. As far as I knew, he was human, but I'd seen him in battle, and he'd give any Traded a run for their money.

He nodded to Clay, then frowned at me. No, not at me. At my sheared horn.

"Who did that to you?" he asked, voice low. Clay shifted. He didn't want me to implicate the Wolf Pack League. But Sonsil would find out, sooner or later.

"I'm not sure who she's working for," I started, making it clear to Clay I wasn't throwing his league under the bus, "but it was Lorna. The woman taken before Ian. She manipulated Glitter, too."

Sonsil seemed to absorb the information for a few moments, his features betraying none of his emotions. But his words did. "You think she has Ian? That he's still alive."

"I do," I said, then I added more softly. "I hope."

"It's okay to believe your friends are still alive, Tira," Sonsil said. "As long as it doesn't blind you to everything else."

There was the reproach.

"Is that…is that it?"

"Is that what?"

"The reproach? For screwing up so badly?"

Sonsil's shoulders seemed to drop. He focused entirely on me, as though purposefully keeping Clay out of our circle. Forcing my attention on him through sheer strength of will. It was a neat trick, really.

"The only thing you screwed up," he said, his voice soft, "was not killing Blake when you had the chance. Hopefully that won't haunt us all."

I must have been tired because tears sprung to my eyes and I swallowed hard. Thankfully, he didn't notice or chose to ignore it.

"Now, come on. We have an operative to save."

3 5

RACHEL HAD BEEN able to quickly determine the location of the corporate headquarters after combining her research with the others'. It was large, square, and in the middle of the seemingly endless industrial district.

The second she was done with it, Sonsil swept up Blake's phone.

"Best not to make the Watch even angrier," Sonsil shrugged.

"I think we might be past that," I said, and Rachel cast a quizzical glance my way. Apparently, the story of my encounter with Blake hadn't traveled very far.

"I wouldn't worry about that," Sonsil said, sounding amused. "When the poor boy woke up, lovely new scar on his face, Dame Zallir and I made sure he knew exactly what would happen if he tried anything like that again. The boy was so scared he cried. But," his look turned dark again, "he will regain his courage. And more than likely, he'll come after you. When he does, make sure you tell us, understood? Segregating you from your guild is how he'll weaken you."

"He already tried again, once," Clay said. Sonsil suddenly seemed taller.

"I'll make sure he regrets that," he clenched his jaw and turned to check on the other operatives. Rachel focused back on her work, frowning at her screen in concentration.

Clay turned to me. "He's pretty cool."

I turned to look at him, surprised. "Sonsil?"

"Yeah, he's got, like, major dad vibes going on. You know, like, you mess with my kids, I'll mess with you?"

"I guess."

"So, like, when do we attack?" Clay asked, shifting again. He was growing bored and restless.

"When we've got enough intel."

"Do we go get it, or what?"

I grinned at him. "We've got operatives on it already, and Rachel is seeing what else she can find."

Rachel heard her name and held up her fingers in a peace sign, but kept concentrating on her work. She dove into various sources to try to uncover as many details as possible about the building.

"The place hasn't been active for a while," she told Sonsil as he returned, "but it's sucking up a hell of a lot of energy. Plus, it has some solar panels, a full parking lot's worth, on its roof.

"Conclusion?" Sonsil asked.

Clay elbowed me and mouthed "dad." I ignored him.

"They're doing something that's drawing a hell of a

lot of energy. Probably producing something? I'm not sure, but I'd certainly love to find out."

"You'll get your chance," he said. "Get ready to head out."

She grinned and gathered her things.

I thought Rachel must have been bored in her previous life on a ship, but she'd helped chart trading passageways and had even figured out different sail systems. and new navigation technology accounting for solar flares. I had no clue what that meant, but it sounded cool.

Girl was pretty damn smart, and Sonsil seemed to have homed in on that, getting her battle training, but also lots of cool gadget and science training that would keep her more explosive tendencies off the battlefield while making full use of her brain.

It was a good tradeoff, overall. Especially after almost being blown up by her several times.

"Clay," Sonsil said. Clay and I stood side-by-side. "I'm glad you'll be here to participate in today's raid. I know that Tira values your friendship. But if you fail to follow our plan or any of my orders, know that you will be the first I'll leave behind."

"Understood," Clay said, and saluted. I groaned.

Sonsil ignored him and focused on me. "Dame Zallir's operatives have scouted as much as they could and retreated. Looks like it's going to be pretty touch and go, so we'll need you and your shadows to provide as much cover as possible."

I nodded. Clay took a protective step toward me. Sonsil sighed.

"Yes, you can be in the first wave, too, Clay." He raised an eyebrow. "We'll need to use someone as a shield."

I was about to protest, but Clay laughed, and Sonsil cracked a smile before walking away. Okay, I was way too on edge, apparently. I looked down at my shaking hand.

"You okay?" Clay asked, concerned. I clasped my hand with my other, soothing it.

"I'm fine," I said. "Too much Tradenaline, not enough sleep."

"You sure?"

"I am. Let's get this done," I started to gather my gear, and turned away, gathering his own. The back of my throat hurt, nausea rolled in my stomach, and my head pounded more than it should.

I'd be fine once we'd entered the fight. I just wanted to get this done. Get Ian, and bring him back.

Safely.

"Tira," Clay said, grabbing my hand as I started walking away. "Can we...I mean...before we head in there..." he looked so unsure of himself that it took me a second to realize he wanted a private word with me. Apparently annoyed with his inability to voice his own thoughts, he pulled me aside, where we could have some privacy.

"Look, I just...I want you to stay near me, okay?"

"We won't leave you behind. Sonsil is good for his word."

"No, I know, but I mean..." he hissed out in frustration and ran his hands over his face like he tried to clear his own mind. "It's just...I heard you scream, Tira." His voice dropped to a shaky whisper. "I was mostly out of it, and I listened to them cut you. Just...I heard you cry, and moan, and scream, and I couldn't...I couldn't get to you..."

"I'm okay," I said, putting a hand on his arm, to convince him of it. "I swear I'm okay."

"I'm supposed to keep you safe," he said softly, then gathered me in his arms and his hug didn't feel awkward. Like he needed to know I was still here.

"I'm okay," I whispered in his ear again and again as I hugged him back, wiping away my tears before he could see them, and letting him hold me as long as he needed to, to convince himself I was still here.

And I wasn't going anywhere.

CLAY LOOKED BEWILDERED as Guild of Shadows operatives worked quickly and seamlessly to infiltrate the building. They scattered, keeping an eye on incoming and outgoing traffic.

With one quick motion of his hand, Sonsil ordered us to move forward. My shadows quickly followed my lead and wrapped around all four of us. My stomach leapt into my throat and I almost threw up, but managed to keep it in. Only Clay seemed to notice, but I motioned that I was fine and we jogged forward.

Three of us moved stealthily to the door while another operative popped it open, moving out of the way. Sonsil indicated for the other operatives to head down the corridor, clearing doors as they went.

The whole place seemed deserted.

We reached the staircase that Rachel had indicated would be at the end of the hall. My control unit flashed. We were to head down. Sonsil quietly sent the signal for other operatives to wait at the top of the staircase until we made sure the way below was clear.

Gorsel cleared the door and we followed. I kept my shadows wrapped around everyone, but the harsh lights hanging from the ceiling above hurt my head, and my control began to slip. I took a deep breath as I followed, managing to hold on to them.

Shit. Too much Tradenaline in my system. The worst part was that I'd take more if I had any left. I was out, which was probably a good thing.

By the time we reached the bottom of the staircase, Sonsil frowned, a quick message flashing on his gaublet. He indicated for us to keep going as he moved back. Clay and I exchanged a look, but we kept going.

Gorsel made short work of the next lock and carefully opened the door. We stepped in, Clay sucking his breath in beside me. We hadn't known what to expect here—the schematics had been unclear. But I certainly hadn't expected this. We were in a massive, circular room extending far above and below us. We'd walked out onto a catwalk that circled the perimeter of the room. Two more similar catwalks above us lined the giant room, and three more spread below us. All surrounding a giant, glowing structure.

A portal. Glowing red in the distance, heat flowed from it. Cooling units stood guard, aimed at its metal frame, which looked about ready to melt regardless.

A quick glance around the room helped me get a sense of our surroundings. The giant portal, which stopped just beneath us and was at least forty feet tall, was surrounded by platforms and large canisters. Those canisters glowed with the same red intensity, and the platforms glowed white at different intervals than the canisters, as though both sources were feeding the portal's energy.

Clay pointed and I followed his finger. No. Not platforms. *Beds.* Metal beds, with people strapped onto them. They were convulsing every time the white energy throbbed, like their very lifeforce powered the portal.

Ian!

"Stay here," I said and, without thinking, I leapt.

From forty feet.

Clay tried to grab my arm as I launched past him, but missed. I think he said my name, but I wasn't sure, focused on getting down there. The other operatives scurried for cover as my shadows abandoned them. I called them beneath me, in the same way I'd pushed Blake back, to support me. And they did, bringing me to a (mostly) soft landing.

The rush cleared my head, which apparently just craved another shot of adrenaline.

Up ahead, battle erupted, guards—and my friends —shouting.

Shit. What the hell had I been thinking? It's like I knew he was probably here and I'd just lost my head. Novice move that would surely get me killed.

I ducked and called my shadows back to me, reaching the first bed. A woman, orange-skinned and sickly looking, stared up at the ceiling. I didn't know if she was still alive, but I figured if I had a chance of saving her and all the others, stopping the big portal was a good idea.

More sounds of battle erupted above me, and a body landed at my feet. I looked, terrified that it might be Clay, but it was a guard, wearing a strange circle symbol above his heart. Another joined him. I glanced up, where Clay was fighting up a storm. He'd teamed up with Gorsel, who'd transformed into his stone state.

I reached down and pulled the wire that connected the woman to the portal. She sighed and closed her eyes. Had I just killed her? I sucked in my own breath at the thought, then saw that she was still breathing.

But the portal hadn't liked losing the connection, apparently. An eerie, haunting screech began to emanate from it, growing in volume.

It was buckling.

Gotta move.

I ran to the second bed and disconnected it, freeing what looked like a blob. When I reached the third bed, purple shadows parted and I came face-to-face with Lorna. Lorna, who could see through my shadows. Lorna, who could control minds.

Her white hair was spread out around her, her eyes dark, focused, and angry.

Something slammed into my head, and I struggled to remain standing. Mustering my strength, I ran towards her in a desperate bid to stop her before she stopped me.

I made it exactly one foot before I was knocked to my knees, my shadows fleeing as hers tried to smother me.

"Tira!" Clay screamed. He appeared at my side, way faster than he should have been able to get there. There was screaming from all around us. Too much screaming.

"Why don't you two talk this out?" Lorna said, and her shadows compressed against my tired, aching mind.

"No," I whispered, calling the shadows back to me, to protect me, and Clay.

She struck sideways and Clay went down. Seeing the opening, I slammed the shadows into her, instead, catching her off balance and knocking her down. Jumping to my feet, I threw two daggers her way, but she nimbly avoided both.

"Lorna!" A voice boomed from the catwalk, and we all looked up to see the Wolf Pack Boss, beside Sonsil, surrounded by fighters. "You can deal with me, or with the Guild of Shadows. Your call."

Clay cheered, and Lorna sneered. "You're all dead."

She threw her strange shadows directly into the catwalk. The metal began to disintegrate. I slammed my own shadows against hers, forcing hers to dissipate, my headache vanishing the more I used my powers, giving me the adrenaline rush my body desperately craved.

"Move!" I screamed to Sonsil and the others. They didn't need any more convincing. They moved quickly off the crumbling platform and onto the next just as something slammed into me.

"You're starting to annoy me," Lorna said, standing over me. I kicked sideways and knocked her down, grabbing her by the collar of her shirt. I hit her, hard, and pulled out a knife, intent on stabbing her eyeball before she could wield her powers again.

But my hand stopped midair, and I couldn't drive the dagger down. My stomach dropped, thinking she held my hand prisoner. She smirked, slipped out of my grasp and punched me in the gut. My breath escaped but I couldn't collapse, held in place by a power I couldn't see.

Not her shadows.

"Tira!" Clay screamed, leaping at Lorna.

She called her shadows and funneled them at Clay, who dodged the blow.

She wasn't the one holding me.

Blake stepped up beside me, wry smile plastered on his stupid face as he looked at Clay avoid another blow from Lorna's growing shadows.

"You're coming with me, demon girl," he said, the cut on his face angry red. I tried to shift and hit him, but I couldn't even talk he held me so tightly. I really, really hated that guy.

And I'd be more than happy to give him more scars. I gritted my teeth and called on my shadows. They heeded me, gathering from every corner. Then something sharp hit my side, and Blake held up a dart. "Thanks for the inspiration," he said, finally turning to look at me. "Time for payback, demon girl."

The sleeping agent washed through me, cold sweat breaking over my body. Clay grunted, but I couldn't turn to see if he was okay. I think I heard Rachel scream.

Don't take me away from here! Everything I needed was right here, including maybe Ian. I struggled against his powers, but the drug robbed me of strength.

If I had Tradenaline, I could fight more. I could stand up against Blake. Help my friends. Instead, I just fought to remain conscious enough to not give the douchebag the satisfaction of seeing me pass out.

He let go of me and I collapsed to my knees.

"Tira!" Clay shouted as guards attacked him. When had guards shown up?

Oh no. I was already losing threads of time, realizing my hands were secured behind my back. Blake was dragging me away.

"Tira!" I thought I heard Clay shouting again. Frustration, anger and angst made his voice sound funny.

"Don't worry about him," Blake said. "He'll have a swifter death than you."

I fought back against slipping away, when I

suddenly fell to the ground. And Dame Zallir stood over me.

"You dare attack an agent of the Watch?" Blake hissed, clutching his bleeding arm.

"I'm sorry, I got confused," she said calmly, though she didn't sheathe the mean looking jagged blade she held. "I figured anyone leaving this battlefield, and taking one of our operatives with them, had to be a bad guy."

Blake actually puffed out his chest, his cheeks splattered with red. "As I've mentioned before, Zallir," I cringed at the lack of title, "we'll deal with rogue Traded how we see fit."

"By attacking them during a battle, like the coward you truly are," she hissed, taking a step toward him, cutting him off from me.

"Don't test me," he said with that damn smirk on his face.

She took another step forward, unaffected by his powers. He looked like he was about to pass out. Well, he wasn't the only one, the room spinning around me.

"That's *Dame* Zallir to you," she said, standing tall.

"I have to bring back the rogue Traded," he said, though he didn't sound nearly as full of it as before. I lowered my head, focused on my breathing and on staying conscious. Trying to hear Clay over the din. Clay would come. He'd take me away. He'd save Ian if I asked real nice, too. That would be amazing.

Dame Zallir's voice snapped me back. "I shall personally bring her to you tomorrow," she said, her frigid voice like cold water on my face. "But now, we need her in this battle."

I focused back on Blake, who gave her a nasty look, hands shaking with rage. But he couldn't stop her, and he knew it.

"If you don't," he spat, "it's *you* we'll come for."

"I would expect as much," she said, giving him a curt nod. "Now, either help, or leave. This is more important than your pettiness."

He shot acid my way and turned on his heel and left. Blake didn't like losing, but I certainly enjoyed watching him lose.

"Now, come, child," Dame Zallir said, freeing my hands. She took out a vicious looking needle and, before the protest could part my lips, plunged it into my heart.

"Time to get back in the battle."

38

I GASPED, the Tradenaline zapping me awake. Clay suddenly crouched near me, covered in gore.

"Are you okay?" he asked, looking like he wanted to murder everything in sight. Dame Zallir had already left and now helped Sonsil fight some of the guards.

"I hate Tradenaline," I mumbled.

"Did Blake hurt you?" he spat.

I shook my head, tasting iron in my mouth. Lorna's shadows grew in the distance, covering the portal and knocking down operatives. Rachel tried to explode, but Lorna's shadows slammed her into a wall. Jombo protected her against the next blow, but she was down.

Damn it.

"We have to stop her," I said, my mind racing from the Tradenaline, my heart lurching at what Dame Zallir had said. She'd hand me to the Watch tomorrow.

If we lived that long, anyway.

Not the time to worry about that. It was time to get back into the game, as Gorsel would so annoyingly put it. I glanced at the mayhem in the room. A circle of dark-red uniformed guards protected Lorna, all Traded with serious judgment issues. The operatives and fighters fought hard against them, to break their line and get to Lorna, whose shadows only continued to grow. The portal pulsed threateningly, waves of red light casting eerie shadows in the room.

The beds surrounding the portal, the ones holding the trapped Traded, glowed with that same light, tubes of light linking each bed to the portal. As though it drained them.

I stood up, Clay steadying me, the Tradenaline sharpening my senses.

Guards screamed as Gorsel rolled over three of them (okay, that was kinda cool).

"We have to stop her," I repeated, willing my mind to slow down long enough to form a plan. Pushing my fears for Ian far below so I could focus on winning the battle. Getting myself killed wouldn't exactly help him.

Lorna's shadows knocked Gorsel sideways, operatives scrambling to get out of his path. Okay, Lorna needed to go first. For her shadows to be broken. And I had the right partner to do that with (sorry, Gorsel).

I shot a grin at Clay. "Distract her, and I'll see if I can mess with those shadows of hers."

"Deal," he said, and we bumped fists as he returned the grin, his entire body vibrating with the need to hit something.

I called my shadows around us as we ran toward to her. She could see through them, but her surrounding guards couldn't. We cleared the few remaining guards and Clay leapt at Lorna, screaming. I focused on her shadows, which were stretched thin as she tried to protect her portal from projectiles.

Her shadows weakened while mine grew plentiful, pulsing with power. I called them from every nook and cranny, promising some fun. They gathered quickly, giddily, responding to my hyped up on Tradenaline powers, and slammed into her shadows so hard they dissipated into dust.

Lorna screamed, three guards turning to attack Clay.

"Clay!" I screamed, pushing my shadows onto one of the guards and shoving him back, giving Clay enough time to turn and engage the other two.

Lorna turned to me, and raised an eyebrow. "You think my shadows are that easy to break?"

I threw a dagger, but before it could hit, her shadows wrapped around me.

Easy trick. I was done with this shit. With these people, and their horn-shearing ways. I called my shadows to push hers away, the Tradenaline beating on my heart like a drum, when her shadows crept to the back of my head. A shiver ran down my spine and, before I could react, they slipped into my mind.

I felt something crack, so deep I could barely hear Clay calling my name.

39

THE GROUND VANISHING. Lorna laughing. The portal so near that my body vibrated, caught in its wake.

Then I stood in another world with Lorna, not filled with vegetation, but with darkness and shadows, vast landscapes riddled with only the light of faraway stars. Soft ground greeted me as I fell to my knees. Sparkling purple water flowed down the flank of a faraway mountain, half of it turning to glittery mist, the other half flowing into a rushing river.

"What is this?" I asked, voice echoing in my own ears, heart aching at the sight of the world surrounding me. The shadows danced, as though they could sense me, unafraid of me. They wanted to be my friends, to carry me through the darkness, to keep me safe, to spend a lifetime forging memories they would remember long after I was gone.

"This is your world," Lorna whispered.

My mouth hung open, tasting the shadows, their thickness and willing spirits. The mountains loomed on the horizon, their shadows as tall as they were. Luminescent flowers bloomed in them, creating their own distinct shadows.

A world for me. A world of shadows and beauty.

I heard laughter and I stood, forgetting Lorna. Children played in the shadows with adults, running through them, using them to fly and vanish, to twirl more quickly or just to rest in. They were all like me. With horns and tails, of all different colors, like whatever light this world held made a rainbow of them.

"Home," I uttered the strange, unfamiliar world.

"All you have to do is help me finish this, Tira, and you can go back home. You'll be loved. Accepted."

A bird, or something like a bird, flew by, shadows draped around it like a winged cloak. Children laughed and helped it reach new heights by teasing its shadows, and it flew higher, its song a gentle breeze.

Home.

"How do you finish this?" I asked, taking a step forward, the ground so soothing and welcoming, every strand of vegetation forming cushioning shadows.

"I just need a bit more time. That's all."

Her voice didn't fit this place. Too jagged in a land of smooth shadows. And it hid more than this land's shadowed depths. Just like her own shadows were different. Maybe from her world, which was why I couldn't touch them.

Not beautiful and shimmering like these.

"You mean kill Ian," my headache returned with a vengeance, and I called to those soft shadows to soothe me. They came, washing over me, though they still felt faraway. A world I couldn't quite reach.

"He's almost dead anyway, Tira. He'll be better off that way, than living in a world that doesn't want him. Or you."

"I want him to stay," I turned to her, hands shaking with fury, wanting to slam her to the ground, to break her and end her.

"You want him to stay?" Lorna said, her voice cruelly mimicking my words. "This is why I sent your explosive friend to kill you, Tira Misu. I knew you'd never let this go." She'd sent Rachel after me. They hadn't been after Aia. Sonsil had suspected all along. He'd wanted to keep me safe, to tell me to be more careful. Not to be seen. Not to be caught.

Lorna huffed and repeated my words again. "*You* want him to stay? Well, *I* want to see my family again!" she screamed. "My children, and my wives! Why was I taken? Why can't I go back, away from this hellish planet that wants us only as slaves! I WANT TO GO HOME!" She shouted, and the world shattered, the beautiful shadows vanishing.

No. A sob caught in my throat at their loss.

Light broke through, but not from earth. Orange light, tinted with yellow pollen which filled the sky. Tall trees surrounded us, small houses built into their trunks, rivers cutting pink streams of thick, viscous liquid through the forest.

"I want to go home," Lorna cried again, looking achingly towards those tree houses. My heart ached for her. And for my own world, which I would never reach.

"This isn't the way," I whispered.

"It's the only way," she said. "I've been here more than forty years, Tira. I've tried everything. There *is* no other way."

"I don't want to lose Ian," I said, feeling numb. She just wanted to go home. That wasn't bad. But she could only do it through killing other Traded. Like Ian. The shadows danced around me, sharpening my focus.

But these shadows were not from the world I longed to belong to, which its shimmering light. They were from Earth, still. My homeworld a vision, or maybe an illusion. *No.* It felt too real.

It was a window. To my real home. To where I'd been born. Where I had a family. Where I'd been loved, and wanted.

A window I could never cross.

And neither could Lorna.

"I'm sorry," I whispered and slammed my shadows into her, sending her flying straight into the portal, disrupting the flow of energy. The whole structure crackled, white and red beams of energy slashing through the entire room.

"It's going to blow!" Rachel screamed.

No no no no! If it blew, it would take Ian with it! It would kill him, before I could save him!

My head pounded, and Clay ran toward me, blood dribbling down his face where he'd been hit. I turned to the portal, instead. I closed my eyes, remembering the shadows of my world.

There were shadows here, too. Shadows that just hadn't been allowed to roam as freely. But they would help me, and I would love them as my own. I reached out for them, all of them, begging them to surround the portal. To absorb its energy. To let it dissolve them, and promising to help them be reborn.

Into something new. Like the shadows from my world. My gut churned and settled. I *knew* this. Even though I hadn't been on my world, seeing it had rekindled a kinship with the shadows that I'd just brushed on before.

I will make you more, I told the shadows, feeling their frantic dance around me. *All you have to do is trust me.*

And they did, gathering around the portal, blocking its wild light. Clay reached me and stopped, looking wide-eyed at the shadows, so thick despite the light.

Then the portal exploded.

40

THE ENERGY of the explosion struck the shadows but they held firm, turning the cascading light into sparkling dust as each shadow captured specks of energy. The structure collapsed, melting into a puddle of metal, only to begin solidifying immediately.

The cooling units kept pumping out air, sending the sparkling shadows swirling up. I smiled and held out my hand, and the not-quite shadows gathered.

"Be free," I whispered, and they danced around me, my hair whipping up before they headed out the door and up the stairway.

Those shadows would never be the same again. I'd have to make sure they were okay.

Later.

"Tira, what was that?" Clay asked, eyes still wide.

I couldn't explain it to him. Clay had always said he'd get me back home. And I'd seen it. I'd *felt* it. And I didn't have the words to explain it to him. Not right now. Instead, I hugged him, taking him by surprise.

His eyes met mine with a question and I smiled at him. "Now, come on, let's find Ian!"

He took a deep, shaky breath. Then he nodded and headed left, while I went right. Sonsil shouted a few orders. The Boss as well. I ignored them all.

They didn't matter. Nothing else mattered. I scrambled across the beds, taking in each face, moving to the next. Operatives swarmed tables as I left them, to treat the wounded and save those who could still be saved.

I held my breath, my heart hammering away their chatter, until I saw him. My breath caught in my throat. He looked sick. Jaundiced. His eyes closed and strained. Pain etched in every feature.

He was still breathing, but every breath rattled.

"Ian," I whispered, leaning over him, gently touching his hair, which was about as out of control as his beard. Others had gathered near, but no one else came close.

His eyes slowly opened. Dark, and deep. There was pain there, and confusion. "Tira?" he croaked out. "I thought you were dead."

He moved his hand as much as he could against the bindings, opening his fist to reveal what he'd been clutching.

My horn. Hooked to the portal, through his holding it. Was that how Lorna had shown me my world? Would she have kept her word? Had she intended to get me back home, too? I ignored the warring emotions and focused on Ian, instead. He was all that mattered. I needed to make sure he was okay.

He was part of my home, here, on this world. The only world I'd ever step foot on. And I couldn't lose him.

"I just had a little accident," I said softly, pointing out my broken horn. That seemed to settle him, and he took a deep breath and closed his eyes, exhaling forcefully as a shockwave of pain rocked his body.

"Ian," I leaned in closer, not knowing how to help.

"I can't shift," he said, his voice strained. "I haven't shifted since they took me."

Sonsil was beside him in an instant, looking for power inhibitors.

"Just hang on, Ian," he said softly, then moved Ian's hair aside to show a black nodule on his neck. He hesitated, but Ian's skin turned ashen, his breath even weaker.

Clay stood behind me, but he might as well have been worlds apart.

I couldn't breathe, slipping my hand into Ian's, willing him to live.

"Ian," Sonsil said, his voice soft but commanding. "I'm going to pull this out, but it's going to hurt. You'll have to shift after, or you'll bleed out."

Ian's lips grew tighter, but he nodded. I squeezed his hand as Sonsil yanked the controller out. It had been linked to his jugular, and crimson blood arced up onto the remains of the portal.

Ian's eyes flew open. He tried to breathe but choked on blood.

"Please shift," I said, leaning over him so that he'd just see me. "Ian, shift now."

His eyes darted sideways and he closed his eyes. It seemed like an eternity passed, but then he began to shift, his muscles and bones rearranging into another form.

"Give the man some privacy!" Sonsil shouted, and the gathered crowd quickly dissipated. "Help the other survivors!"

I kept an eye on Ian until he was finished shifting, into a tiny gray mouse. I picked him up. He shook his fur and looked at me, deep eyes piercing my soul.

"Hello, you," I grinned. "Want to get some rest in my pouch?" He nodded and I gently put him in my pouch, where he settled down. Shifting would allow him to heal. His body, at least.

His mind and heart would take a lot more time. If they'd ever truly mend.

"He's okay?" Sonsil asked, looming over me. I resisted the urge to take a step back.

I opened the pouch and he peeked in, his shoulders noticeably dropping.

"Well done," he said, his voice thick with emotion, before he quickly turned away to check on the other survivors.

I couldn't stop smiling, though I felt exhausted.

Clay saw my smile, but he didn't return it as he walked up to me. Seeing the look in his dark eyes, my smile faded, too.

And I held my breath again.

41

"THE WOLF PACK IS LEAVING," Clay said as he stepped up beside me. Behind him, survivors were being gently lifted up, to be brought to safety and healing. The portal pieces gathered and dissected, for study.

Lorna's body was nowhere to be found. Part of me hoped she'd made it home, somehow. That she'd found her family, and some peace.

Another part of me really hoped she'd died. Painfully.

Clay paused, then looked away, like he didn't want to look me in the eye. "I think it's time I get back to my own people," he said, a dagger in my heart. "It's okay," he said, like he had to explain anything at all.

"Clay…"

"Look, I get it. He's your friend."

"So are you," I whispered. "Clay…"

"I know I am. And I think we'll always be friends," the hurt in his voice nearly cut me in two. "But, think on it, Tira. I wanted you to leave the Guild of Shadows for me. And you didn't." He held up his hand to stop my protests, which I wasn't sure I could have blurted out around the lump in my throat anyway. "But you left it for *him*."

He paused, adjusted his weapons, and locked eyes with me. "I just…I just hate that he gets to be there for you and I don't, you know?"

"Clay," I wanted to say something. Anything. To take his pain away. To let him know how loved he was. How much he meant to me. How I wouldn't have survived this far without him.

"It's Claws, now," he said, his voice finding strength. "Voted by the public, for my next match. Guess we all have to find our place eventually." He turned on his heel and left.

And my barely rebuilt heart cracked into a thousand pieces again.

Dame Zallir waited for me near Ian's room, hands behind her back. Sonsil, who had taken up escort duty, nodded to her.

"I'll take Ian in," he said, holding out his hand. I hesitated for a split second, then reluctantly gave him the pouch. "I promise I'll stay with him."

"Okay."

He stared at me, as though studying my worth. Then he nodded, and walked into Ian's room, cradling the pouch like he cradled his own heart.

"The Guild of Shadows was formed with a very specific purpose in mind, Tira," Dame Zallir said as soon as the door closed behind him.

"To maintain the balance, I know." I just wanted to go in there and make sure Ian was okay. I didn't want to leave now. To be taken to the Watch. I was too tired to fight, or run. My heart ached, and so did my body, the Tradenaline leaving me shaky.

"Indeed," she said, "but not in the way Sonsil

believes."

That made me pause. I narrowed my eyes. "Who are you? And what is your connection with the Guild?"

A wry smile graced her lips. "That doesn't matter," she said. "What matters is the balance."

"What is maintaining the balance, if not stopping rogue Traded?" That had been a trap. To see if she'd deny it. But she didn't.

"It's the balance of powers," she said. "There are certain Traded too dangerous to ever see the light of day. Who could do more damage than even they themselves understand."

I stared at her, my head not quite wrapping around what she was saying. "You know Gorsel just basically turns into a rock, right?"

Steel coated her laugh. "Yes. And you wrap shadows. And Jombo is a giant lizard. Power isn't just about ability, Tira. And damage isn't just physical. A lizard replacing the heir to a throne is best forgotten in darkness. Best to let the rumors grow without proof to substantiate them. What if they say he should be heir?"

"Jombo is heir to a throne?"

"It's just an example," she said, though I wasn't convinced. "All these children marked for death, Tira. The Guild of Shadows took them all to make them useful, but also to keep them out of the light. Traded that are too recognizable, or that could shift some political power. It's a fine balance, we maintain."

"By staying in the shadows."

"Exactly," she hesitated, then shook her head. "But powers shift. Balance topples. Needs change. And, sometimes, even those who prefer to stay in darkness must step into the light. That is also the power of the Guild of Shadows. And that's what I bring that Sonsil can't. The light."

"Are you going to hand me to the Watch?" I asked, hating how weak and tired my voice sounded. How scared.

She looked at me with warmth in her eyes for a second.

"There is a way to stop the Watch from claiming you, Tira Misu, but only if you are brave enough."

She paused and waited for my answer.

"I don't know if I have much bravery left," I mumbled, "but I really would prefer staying with the Guild of Shadows."

She smiled, lines gathering at her eyes. "And the Guild of Shadows would like you to stay, as well." That made me feel kinda good. But all I really wanted to do was sleep with Ian curled at my feet, for as long as the world let me. Except I knew the world wasn't that nice.

"Now, go," Dame Zallir said, as though willing energy into me. "Gather your strength and courage. Go speak to Aia."

Why Aia? The question nearly escaped my lips, but Dame Zallir cut me off. "Time is short and precious before the Watch comes knocking."

I nodded, gutted I had to leave Ian again so soon. And tell Aia I'd lost her tablet. And also not get to nap. Only the thought that this might stop Blake from getting his hands on me made my feet move away from Dame Zallir.

Her words followed me down the hall, though, making everything much more mysterious. And even less appealing.

"It's time you stepped out of the shadows, Tira Misu."

4 3

AN HOUR LATER, I slipped into Aia's study, not bothering with my shadows. She paced the room, arms behind her back. She'd wear a hole in her pretty rug if she kept it up. She stopped when she saw me, a nervous smile on her face until she spotted my missing horn.

"You're hurt," she said, real concern lacing her words.

"Who are you?" I asked softly.

Aia sat down, and suddenly looked much older than I'd believed her to be earlier. Like a great weight had landed on her shoulders. Or an old wound had been reopened.

"I'm no one, really. But I used to be a mother," her words grew so soft I strained to hear. "Over twenty years ago, my baby vanished. In its place was a monster. Or, what I thought was a monster." I sat before her, held prisoner by her words.

"My father whisked it away, to contacts in the city. I never saw that baby again. Or mine."

She stood up, like she couldn't stand to look at me anymore.

"I carried that guilt for a long time, and funneled it into trying to establish better laws and protection for the Traded. But people were afraid, and blamed the helpless children for the loss of our own. Still, I kept pushing, sharing the story of that baby, of my shame, and my guilt."

She took a portrait from the buffet and handed it to me. A baby girl, laughing, dark skin glowing, a full head of tight curls.

"My daughter's name was Amelia. *Is* Amelia. I have to believe she's found a good home, on a faraway world. That her parents were kinder than I was."

"You can't blame yourself for that," I said, remembering my own shitty foster parents. "You lost a baby, too."

"I did, and you're kind to say that," Aia whispered. "But I also gave one up that day, and it took me years to find her again. I've been trying even harder to dissolve the guilds since then. To get her freed from a system I helped put her in. But the Watch pushed back, not wanting to let one of the Traded go, for fear it would rip apart the careful system they'd established. And no matter how hard I pushed, they pushed harder. Until an old friend decided to help me out by putting my daughter in my path, and let the fates do what they would."

I couldn't speak as she looked up at me.

"She was memorable, that baby I gave up, you see," she took a deep, rattling breath. "Purple skin. Horns. A tail. I thought Amelia had been killed by a demon, Tira. I'm so sorry. I shouldn't have just given you up. If I can find any way to make it up to you, I swear I will."

My mind blanked for a few moments, before being assailed by images. Of my foster family hating me. Giving me up as soon as they could. And they hadn't even been the first to give me up. I looked across the room to her and stood up.

True, she looked older. But I could still see the young mother in her eyes. The mother who'd lost her baby. And, in her grief, given up the monster who'd replaced her.

I understood that. I got the pain she must have felt. And, more than that, I believed her when she said she'd looked for me. She'd tried to make the world a better place for people like me.

Like Sonsil had looked for me. And Clay. Like I'd looked for Ian. What was family if not the people who never gave up on us?

"I saw my home world, I think," I was pretty sure Lorna hadn't lied to me. Not with the emotions it had elicited in me. A world all my own, where I belonged. Where I had family. Just like Lorna had had hers, and had been desperate to reach them. Aia slowly stood up, hanging on my every word, eyes wide as though terrified of what I might reveal.

"It was beautiful, and kind," I whispered, remembering the shadows. The laughter. And how much I wanted to be a part of it. "Colorful, and full of life. I like to think your daughter's enjoying my world, and that it's kind to her."

Aia nodded, her eyes bright with tears. She swallowed hard. "Kinder to her than this world has been to you."

I crossed the gulf of sorrow between us and gathered her in my arms, holding her as she finally let go of the grief and guilt she'd held on to for far too long.

Maybe I didn't mind hugs so much, after all.

EPILOGUE

Sonsil sat in Ian's room, arms crossed, looking down. He seemed relieved to see me.

"He won't change," he said. "I don't know if it's trauma-induced, or what they did, but he's not changing."

"Sometimes, he can't quite change at will," I said, hoping to make him feel better. "Like when he was stuck as a snail."

Sonsil chuckled. "It took me forever to figure out if it was him or not. I lived in fear of stepping on him."

He laughed at the memory, finding comfort in it. Sonsil wasn't young, he had the same lines as Aia. Maybe he'd lost a kid, too. Maybe Ian had replaced the child he'd lost. I didn't feel comfortable asking.

"I'll stay with him. He might just need to be reminded he's not alone," my voice softened. "We all need to be reminded of that, some days."

He looked down at me, as though seeing me for the

first time. "We do," he said. "Thank you. Let me know if anything changes."

"Something did change," I whispered. His head snapped to the cave, but then slowly turned back to me. I pushed on. "I met the mom whose baby I replaced." I forced myself to maintain eye contact, to see if I could spot a lie. "She says a friend put me in her path."

He nodded. "Dame Zallir."

I'd expected another lie, and was surprised to hear the truth. I wanted to know who she was. What she was doing here. Why she'd done what she had. But I knew I wouldn't get those answers.

Instead, I asked the one question I thought I might get an answer to.

"What happens now?"

He leaned forward, voice low as he spoke. "Tomorrow morning, before the Watch comes knocking, you'll head back to the embassy," I hung on his every word, like my life depended on it. Which, technically, it really did. "The ambassador has called a press conference. Where he'll introduce you to the world as his lost grandchild, and how he's trying to pave a way to the future of the Traded by reconnecting with you."

My mind stayed stuck, not able to fully comprehend his words. Blame the fear, the exhaustion, or the Tradenaline crash, but I just stared at Sonsil, blinking slowly.

"Did you hear me, Tira?"

"You want me to…to hide in the shadows and keep them safe?"

Sonsil gave a low chuckle and shook his head. "I told Dame Zallir you might choose to give yourself up to the Watch instead of following this plan." He grew serious again and sighed. "Look, I know this isn't ideal, but you'll have to step onto the podium with the ambassador. So he can introduce you."

More blinking from me.

Another sigh from Sonsil. Clay was right. He really was like a dad.

Clay. Thinking of him made me even more tired and sad.

"I know you hate the light, Tira," Sonsil said softly, misinterpreting at least part of my worry. "And I'd much prefer you stayed in the shadows. But you need to be recognizable. To be someone people care about, so that the Watch won't be able to touch you. There's power in the light, Tira. There's power in being known. In being someone people care about."

Clay cared about me. And he stepped into the light of the arena every day. He was known, and loved, and people voted on a cool name for him. And yet they hoped he'd die, too, so they could win some money.

I didn't think the light would save me, no. But I also knew the shadows couldn't protect me anymore.

I swallowed hard and nodded. What else could I do?

He stood up, and so did I.

"I'm sorry, Tira," he said, and I thought he meant it. "For now, just…rest. Give Ian the space he needs to heal, and remind him he's not alone. I'll be back first thing in the morning. I won't let you go alone, I promise."

I felt a bit better for that, but not much.

"Thanks," I mumbled. He nodded and stepped out. I stood there, trying to free my numb mind from its fear. Breathing proved impossible, coming in short gasps as my heart hurt, my entire chest on fire. Maybe I'd get a heart attack and I wouldn't have to step onto that stage tomorrow.

The very thought of it made me dizzy and I lowered myself to the ground, clutching my knees to my chest and lowering my head on them, wishing I could hide here, forever. Away from the light. Away from people, and expectations.

Tomorrow, everyone will know a purple demon lives on their world. Everyone will look at me. Everyone will know my name.

My head spun and tiny sobs started to escape. I couldn't stop them, like my breath decompressed out of me. Too much Tradenaline. Not enough sleep. Too many damned emotions.

A whine caught my ear and I shifted my head, seeing the familiar face of Max (aka Ian in dog form) beside me, dark eyes drooping and worried.

I laughed between sobs. "You shouldn't be worried about me. *I'm* worried about *you*."

He licked my hand and sat beside me. I wrapped my arms around him, the familiar fur comforting. My legs unfurled and I leaned into him, and he leaned into me.

I still felt like shit, but I didn't feel alone, anymore.

And I thought, from the way he fell asleep, letting me use him as a pillow, that Ian felt much the same, too.

As his breaths lengthened and I started to drift off, my resolve grew. I'd step into the light, tomorrow. Not because I wanted to. I'd face my fears so that I could come back here, in the shadows.

So that I could come back safely to the place I was finally willing to call home.

- The End -

Marie Bilodeau is an Ottawa-based author and storyteller, with eight published books to her name. Her speculative fiction has won several awards and has been translated into French (Les Éditions Alire) and Chinese (SF World). Her short stories have also appeared in various anthologies. In a past life not-so-long ago, she was Deputy Publisher for The Ed Greenwood Group (TEGG). Marie is also a storyteller and has told stories across Canada in theatres, tea shops, at festivals and under disco balls. She's won story slams with personal stories, has participated in epic tellings at the National Arts Centre, and has adapted classical material.

Marie is co-host of the Archivos Podcast Network with Dave Robison, co-chair of Ottawa's speculative fiction literary convention CAN-CON with Derek Künsken, and is a casual blogger at Black Gate Magazine.

Find out more and see pretty book covers at www.mariebilodeau.com.